PLAIN SURVIVAL

ALISON STONE

TREEHAVEN PRESS

All rights reserved.

No part of this book may be reproduced in any form or by any electronic or mechanical means, including information storage and retrieval systems, without written permission from the author, except for the use of brief quotations in a book review.

> PLAIN SURVIVAL
> Treehaven Press
> Copyright © 2021 by Alison Stone

This book is a work of fiction. The names, characters, places, and incidents are products of the writer's imagination or have been used fictitiously and are not to be construed as real. Any resemblance to persons, living or dead, actual events, locale or organizations is entirely coincidental.

Be the first to learn about new books, giveaways, and deals by signing up for Alison's newsletter on her website: https://alisonstone.com/newsletter

Rev. C

❦ Created with Vellum

CHAPTER 1

Deputy Caitlin Flagler pulled into the parking lot at the fire station, surprised by the number of horses and buggies lined up. Apparently the Amish had set aside their dislike of law enforcement to join against a potential common enemy: the preppers group that had taken up residence in Hunters Ridge a little more than a year ago. Even though Caitlin couldn't see the attraction of living like the world was about to come to an end, she wasn't convinced they were doing anything wrong, unless she counted the undue influence on the young men—both Amish and *Englisch*—in the community.

It seemed in the eyes of the strict Amish families whose sons were drawn by the easy money and freewheeling lifestyle that Clyde Wheeler was the devil come to their sleepy town.

Caitlin put her patrol car into park, adjusted the collar on her thick winter coat, and climbed out, bracing herself against the arctic January wind. Despite being a lifelong resident of Hunters Ridge, she'd never get used to the bone-chilling cold that settled in this time of year and made a person wonder if they'd ever enjoy another gorgeous summer.

The gravel crunched under her boots as she made her way to the double glass doors of the fire hall. Most of the folding chairs were already occupied. The large gymnasium of sorts had seen its share of pickup basketball games, wedding receptions, and, of course, town meetings. Caitlin had planned to get here before the meeting started so she could study the faces of everyone who arrived, but she had been held up after she got a call from dispatch that a newly licensed driver had overcompensated on an icy curve and ended up in a snowy ditch. Fortunately, the only thing injured was the teen's pride in front of a girl he had been trying to impress and had instead given the scare of her life. His old car might be a total loss, too. The tow truck driver had been busy because of the road conditions, and now Caitlin was late.

Now, all she could do was scan the back of the crowd, unable to distinguish one broad-brimmed hat, bonnet, and winter cap from the next. She had been very curious who was tied to the compound on the ridge. Or were most of these people assembled merely interested in more information?

"You should know better than anyone what it means to have privacy." Sheriff Littlefield leaned heavily on a podium. The middle-aged man rarely got out from behind his desk, and his sedentary lifestyle was catching up to him. If he ever needed to give chase out in a field, his heart might not be able to take it. "By all accounts, Clyde Wheeler purchased the property on Cow Lick Road and gathered a few families to create a self-contained community. We're not in the business of policing the activities of your sons." His tone was thick with condescension.

The sheriff liked to run his mouth. To convince others

that his thinking was the right way, even if others might not agree. His height, heft and position gave him a lot of sway. Not many people were up to challenging him. She supposed that was why he had been repeatedly reelected as sheriff.

Caitlin wasn't so sure the sheriff's "hands-off approach" was a good call in this instance. She and many of the other deputies had referred to individuals living on the property, with its barbed-wire fence, gate across the driveway, and constant construction, as doomsday preppers. Considering the world at large, she supposed no one could fault them, but it still felt extreme, especially out here in the country. What did they have to protect? To hide? Caitlin walked along the back of the crowd, then made her way up the left side. Only a couple of the Amish women turned their heads to take note of her. The Amish men, mostly older, seemed angry, as if these newcomers had encroached on their land. Land that had previously belonged to Old Man Hershberger, whose family had moved to Pennsylvania to an Amish community in communion with Hunters Ridge. Rumors suggested Wheeler had outbid an Amish family for the prized land on the ridge.

"They're luring our young men away from the farm with promises of money." That from Abram Troyer. Caitlin knew most of the residents by name. "There must be something you can do. There're trucks going in and out of there at all hours." He should know. His farm was just south of the property. One of his dogs had been hit by a driver barreling down the country road.

Caitlin paused when she got to the front of the gymnasium, but stopped short of joining her boss near the podium. Even though she worked for the sheriff, she liked to maintain some separation in hopes the Amish who were already leery of law enforcement might feel she was approachable. She knew it was a long shot.

"Hey there." Her friend and coworker Deputy Olivia Kincaid sat in the front row, pushing a baby buggy gently back and forth, back and forth. Olivia was dressed in civilian clothes and had never looked happier. The new mother slanted a smile at her and took the diaper bag off the seat and patted it. "Take a load off. Something hold you up?"

"Some poor kid lost control of his car on the curve out on Route 78," she whispered as she sat down. Olivia winced. "He's okay, but can't say the same about the car."

"Littlefield's not in a good mood." Olivia leaned in close and spoke softly, seeming to take delight in their boss's aggravation. "He thinks this town meeting is total BS. He still wants to maintain a hands-off approach to Wheeler's group."

"He's not very good at hiding how he feels." Caitlin shifted in her seat and looked casually over her shoulder, scanning the faces of the residents. "I'd think he'd tone down the attitude a bit to get some cooperation from the Amish instead of their usual silence."

"You'd think," Olivia deadpanned. She leaned forward and checked on her beautiful daughter, who was sleeping through the most excitement this town had seen since a stalker had the residents of quiet Hunters Ridge locking their doors.

"Hey, what are you doing here, anyway?" Caitlin dipped her head and caught a peek at the sleeping baby, too. "You wouldn't catch me here if I didn't have to be." She suspected that wasn't exactly true. Being a deputy was her life, even if she had to deal with the likes of Sheriff Littlefield.

"Trust me, when you're stuck at home 24/7 in the middle of winter, you'll be looking for excuses to get out," Olivia said. "I wouldn't trade Charlotte for the world, but she's not the best conversationalist."

"Ha ha." Caitlin reached into the stroller and tucked the silky fabric of the blanket under her goddaughter's chin. She didn't consider herself maternal, but boy, she could have eaten that precious girl up.

Movement out of the corner of her eye drew her attention. Deputy Dylan Kimble strolled in late, taking the same path as she had to the front of the gymnasium. Her friend leaned toward her, bumping her shoulder. "I see Dylan's back from his honeymoon. After today's meeting, he'll feel like he never left."

"Speaking of vacations, when do you plan on returning to work?" Caitlin touched the bar of the stroller.

"Oh, sweet, naïve Caitlin. I'm not on vacation. I don't think I've ever been so sleep-deprived."

Heat crawled up her neck and she laughed awkwardly. "Of course, I didn't mean, I just—"

Olivia squeezed her knee. "I'm teasing you." She pulled her hand away and resumed pushing the stroller back and forth, back and forth. "Drew and I have been discussing my return. Maybe this summer."

Something in the downturn of Olivia's mouth made Caitlin ask, "You're coming back, right?" She was careful to keep her voice low as the sheriff took questions from the anxious residents of Hunters Ridge. The din of discontent around them drowned out their quiet conversation. "I can't be the only one left." She and Olivia were the only two female deputies in the department.

"I never thought I'd feel this way, but after becoming a mom…" Olivia looked at Caitlin and her cheeks infused with pink. "Well, I'm considering my options. Drew and I will reevaluate in the spring."

Caitlin smiled, but her heart dropped. "I'm sure you'll figure out what's best for you." She couldn't help but wonder about their friendship going forward. She'd been a good friend, but now that Olivia was a wife and mother, they had yet another thing not in common. Caitlin didn't allow herself to wonder what it would be like to have a family of her own. A husband. A baby.

The sheriff cleared his throat, and Caitlin glanced toward the podium. The sheriff shot them a hard gaze, and Caitlin felt like she was in high school. She straightened her back and tuned into the sheriff. She shifted in her seat to check out those in attendance again. Half the audience was Amish, and the other people lived in town. She recognized most—if not all—of the faces, even if she stumbled over a few of their names.

"Someone has to get in there and see what they're up to. My Fletcher goes up there and comes back with more money than he knows what to do with," one concerned Amish woman said, glancing around to a few bobbing heads of affirmation. "He has a car now"—then, as if realizing that she was telling stories outside school, she lifted her hand in the general direction of the bishop—"but he's still on Rumspringa." She slid to the front of her chair and squared her shoulders, as if getting a second wind. "If we let outsiders negatively influence our sons…" She shook her head, and Caitlin could only imagine how hot the woman was under the thick black bonnet. "We just can't."

The din of chatter grew louder, and the sheriff had to slap his palm on the podium to get their attention. "Mrs. Yoder"—Caitlin was impressed that he knew her name because he usually dismissed the Amish—"there is no sign that they're doing anything illegal."

"What about the Miller boy?" a man hollered from the back row, his eyes shadowed by his broad-brimmed hat. Unrest rolled over the crowd. This was the real reason the Amish were here in large numbers. Their sons being lured by the evil of excess was one thing, but ending up dead in the woods was another altogether.

"Now, now." The sheriff held up his meaty hand. "Sadly,

Aaron Miller died in a hunting accident. I looked at the M.E. report myself. I believe the Bible says something about gossip."

Embarrassment and anger threaded up Caitlin's spine. The sheriff probably couldn't quote one Bible passage, but he was manipulative enough to use their beliefs to shame them.

He grabbed both sides of the lectern. "We can't have any kind of vigilante justice."

"The Amish are hardly the type to seek retribution, Sheriff Littlefield." The elderly bishop pushed up on his cane and stood in the front row. "That's why we need support from the sheriff's department."

"You have our support." Littlefield cast a smug look. "Aaron Miller was out hunting a few days past shotgun season. We're not looking to make this harder than it has to be."

"He's dead," a young Amish woman said about halfway back. "Nothing you can do to him now." The older woman next to her scowled and reached over, effectively shushing her.

"Tragic." Sheriff Littlefield bowed his head in a gesture that seemed less than sincere. "The sheriff's department will investigate any wrongdoing, but that's not what this was."

"What about all the trucks going in and out of the property at all hours?" another disembodied male voice asked.

Deputy Kimble took a step forward, his thumbs hooked into his utility belt. "I've talked to Clyde Wheeler on many occasions. They're doing a lot of construction. They're bringing supplies in." Caitlin made a mental note to talk to her fellow deputy about this. The preppers group had been fodder for gossip since they arrived about a year ago, the subject of grumbling from the Amish who hated to see their sons get involved in an insular group that wasn't their own. But only after the Miller kid's death did it become a genuine

7

concern of the community that forced the sheriff to call a town meeting. "Mr. Wheeler believes most of the work will be completed by spring."

"I'll believe that when I see it," another resident mumbled.

"There's nothing illegal going on," the sheriff said. "Let's show them what good neighbors we can be."

Caitlin shifted in her seat to study the faces behind her. The deep lines of anger on Abram Troyer's face were replaced by something else, perhaps shame. Or was it disgust? If the sheriff didn't quell their concerns, they might strain the Amish's usual restraint.

She searched for Aaron's parents. The young man had gone missing two weeks ago, only to be found in the woods by a search party with his hunting rifle at his side. Her mind flashed back to the night her mother had gone missing…

The hours of waiting…until she was notified about her mother's accident. Her death. A rush of heat washed over her. She blinked a few times as the Amish hats and bonnets blended together like waves bobbing in a black sea.

"Are you okay?" Olivia asked, her voice sounding like it was coming from the other side of a long tunnel.

Caitlin pulled at her collar and unzipped her jacket. "I'm going to step outside. It's hot in here." Concern flashed across her friend's face, but Caitlin waved her off. "No, no, stay here, it's too cold for the baby." She patted the handle of the stroller as tiny dots danced in her field of vision.

"Come over for dinner tomorrow night, okay? I miss you." Olivia smiled.

"Of course." Caitlin returned her smile despite the pinpricks of heat washing over her. She hurried toward the exit. She should have eaten breakfast before her shift, she reasoned. Stepping outside, she inhaled greedy gulps, grateful, for once, that the air was icy.

More than a decade since her mother's tragic death, she

was surprised by the sudden onslaught of emotions the trigger of a memory could produce.

"You okay?" a male voice asked from far away, or maybe not that far away. Everything still seemed a little distorted.

Caitlin quickly straightened, not wanting anyone to witness a deputy—especially a female deputy—in a weak position. She waved her hand, even though she still felt icky. "Fine, thanks." She turned to see penetrating brown eyes under a black knit hat studying her carefully.

He tilted his head and concern softened his features. "You look a little pale," he said.

Caitlin had heard that more times than she cared to count. Having red hair and a fair complexion were nothing new. "That's my normal coloring, but thanks for noticing," she shot back, trying to act casual.

"Well, if you're sure…" His smooth voice trailed off, and he ran his hand down his shaggy brown beard. The penetrating gaze of his warm brown eyes sparked something deep inside her that she immediately brushed aside. She had never been partial to guys with beards.

His thick wavy hair trimmed short at the sides and the sharp planes of his face made her want to make an exception.

Perhaps the heat had affected her more than she had realized.

He turned to walk away when Caitlin thought to call after him. "Hey, I didn't catch your name." She needed to note strangers in town, considering the unrest over the preppers' compound on the ridge. At least, that was the lie she told herself.

Without turning around he hollered, "I didn't give it to you."

CHAPTER 2

Austin Young—at least to those he had introduced himself to in Hunters Ridge—strode to his truck parked behind the long row of buggies. If someone had told him a year ago he'd be living among the Amish in a town he had never heard of, he would have informed them that they were a few cards short of a full deck. He hunched his shoulders against the stiff wind and resisted the urge to turn around to catch another glimpse of the deputy. Her pale coloring and the way she tugged at her coat collar worried him. Was she having a medical emergency? Their quick exchange assured him she was most likely fine, but he feared he had suddenly drawn a sheriff's deputy's attention.

When he reached his pickup with a snowplow mounted to the front, he risked a look back toward the fire hall. The sidewalk where the deputy had stood was now empty. He ran a hand over his beard, damp from cold and condensation, then slid behind the wheel.

Seemed he wasn't the only one interested in what Clyde Wheeler was doing in the compound up on the ridge. He just hoped he'd uncover the truth before Clyde and his buddies realized what he was up to. He needed answers.

Austin made his way out of the parking lot, careful to give the horses a wide berth. He adjusted the heating vents and wondered how the Amish handled the cold in their buggies. He was drumming his fingers on the steering wheel, debating his next move, when it was decided for him. A familiar orange clunker sat in the gravel lot of the bar across from the cheese factory. He pulled in, parked next to it, then braced himself to play the game that was growing old.

The bar smelled like most dark and dank bars in small towns: of cold beer and quiet desperation. Austin never understood the need to buy his drinks at a watering hole when the local grocery store and his comfy couch were more appealing. But the people he needed to talk to weren't the kind he cared to invite in for a Buffalo Bills or Sabres game.

Not if he could help it.

Austin slid up to the bar and got the attention of the bartender, an older man who he had learned was looking to sell the joint and move someplace warmer, but there weren't many investors eager to invest in an old building and a struggling business. So, here he was, night after night—except Sunday, when everyone, even the rebels, seemed to follow the Sabbath—popping bottle caps and sliding bottles across the smooth bar to whoever was willing to pay twice the price for what the small grocery store or gas station was selling in multiples of six.

"Hey, Duke," Austin said, always wondering if that was a first or last name, but he decided it didn't matter since the information he got from the man was the same, regardless.

The old man with a grizzled face and beefy hands grabbed Austin's beer of choice, popped the cap and slid it down the smooth wood with a familiar greeting. This time it was about the weather.

Austin nodded and took a long sip, aware of the young men sitting near him, even if he wasn't looking directly at them. It took only half a bottle before Elmer Graber joined him, no doubt sniffing around for a free drink. Austin lifted his finger to Duke, who produced a fresh bottle for his friend. If you could call him that.

Austin waited a respectable time before saying, "I hear the locals want to run Clyde out of town." That might have been overstating the message, but he wanted to gauge Elmer's reaction.

"Not gonna happen," the kid said. "Ain't doing anything to get run out of town for. Besides…" He puffed up his chest, then the air seemed to go out of him, perhaps deciding against telling him whatever he was about to say.

Austin cut him a sideways glance, curious about how much the kid knew. Austin had been singlehandedly investigating them for six weeks and had found enough suspicious activity to raise several red flags with the local authorities, or even the FBI, if that had been his intention. He didn't trust the local sheriff, and he *was* the FBI. But he wasn't at a point in his investigation to go to his supervisor with what he had uncovered. An uneasiness settled in his gut. He could lose his job over his need to play fast and loose with the rules.

Austin did push the kid. "I imagine the Amish folks are unhappy their sons are getting caught up with outsiders."

Elmer took another long swig of his beer and laughed. "You don't know the half of it."

Austin set his bottle down and rested his elbow on the counter. "You told me you grew up Amish."

Again, the laugh.

"So why stick around Hunters Ridge? Why not get the heck out of town?" He studied the kid's face and for the first time his mask of bravado slipped, then immediately reappeared.

Elmer's lips slanted in a smirk, as if he had the world figured out. "Not much for a guy with an eighth-grade education out there." He tilted his head toward the doors, and the cheese factory across the street. Austin had learned Elmer used to work there before taking up with the compound. "I got a decent job. Friends." He shrugged. "No one will guilt me into leaving town."

Austin let it go. He had befriended a few young men at the bar when he first arrived and had decided Elmer was his best bet into the compound. The kid had nerve, but he also had a needy way about him. Austin was working a few angles, and he had a strong suspicion that Elmer wanted to be the one to be a big hero in Clyde Wheeler's eyes. He just hoped he could exert more influence over Elmer than that Solomon Redman kid who was major trouble. Austin was still digging up information to find out how big of a problem he was.

"Well," Elmer said, standing then teetering. "I gotta go."

Austin stood. "Hey, why don't you let me drive you home?"

Elmer blinked slowly. "I've got my car."

Austin laughed, trying to downplay how much he despised drunk drivers. "Not a good idea." He wasn't sure appealing to Elmer's common sense would be effective.

The Amish kid's shoulders came down, as if he was considering it.

Austin pressed. "I'll drop you off this evening. Swing you back by to get your car tomorrow. You don't want to risk it, man." Not again.

Elmer nodded. "*Yah*, you're probably right."

The two men stepped out into the chilly afternoon, their breaths coming out on vapor clouds. "I'm over here." Austin directed Elmer over to his truck and opened the passenger door. "Home?"

"*Neh*, the compound."

Excitement sparked in Austin's gut. The compound. He jammed the truck into drive. "Working on a Saturday?"

Elmer scrubbed a hand over his patchy beard. Austin had heard that only married men in the Amish community grew beards, but he supposed Elmer wasn't much into the rules. Austin cut him a sideways glance. Elmer had his elbow resting on the door and looked like he might say something, but stopped short of giving Austin anything useful. "Just work stuff."

They headed up to the compound and Austin was forced to drop his new friend off outside the gates. This was as close as he'd get. For now. Elmer muttered his goodbyes and pushed out the door, leading with his shoulder.

After Elmer shuffled up the lane and talked to the guard, the man opened the gate, casting a suspicious gaze toward his truck. Austin lifted his hand to partially block his face, but he suspected someone was already running his plates caught on the camera mounted on a nearby tree. Austin waited a beat, as if he was just making sure his friend made his way up the driveway, then after getting as good a look as he'd ever get from this angle, he reversed his truck out of there. That was the closest he had been able to get to Clyde Wheeler, but he had a good feeling—if he could call the constant buzz of anticipation a "good feeling"—that he'd be welcomed inside the gates. Soon.

And that would be Wheeler's biggest mistake.

CHAPTER 3

The humming noise of her cell phone vibrating on Caitlin's bedside table woke her out of a mostly dreamless sleep, punctuated by the handsome face of the man she had encountered outside the fire hall earlier that day. She inwardly groaned at being woken up and at her seemingly baseless infatuation with a stranger.

She really needed to put herself out there more if she didn't want to be the woman with twelve cats in her old age. But the pickings were slim in a small town, especially for a woman in law enforcement. That intimidated most men. And Caitlin Flagler—unlike her mother—wasn't inclined to hook up with anyone.

A sliver of shame nudged her conscience. She shouldn't think poorly of the dead. Especially her mother.

Muttering to herself, she slipped her arm out from under her cozy warm quilt and palmed her phone. Even before she opened her eyes and squinted at the screen in the heavily shadowed bedroom, she knew it could only be one person.

The caller ID confirmed it.

"'Lo." Caitlin croaked out the second syllable of her half-hearted, middle-of-the-night greeting.

"Sorry to wake you, sweetie." Wanda Reynolds' raspy voice sounded across the line. Caitlin always suspected her dear friend took the worst shift possible so she could sneak in a cigarette or two right at her workstation when smoking inside was strictly forbidden. Caitlin had caught the cloying scent still floating in the air occasionally when she stopped by dispatch. She loved everything about this woman except her hard to give up habit. Wanda had been like a mother figure to Caitlin, the only reason she allowed her to call her "sweetie" and get away with it. If a male cohort dared to, she would have throat-punched him.

Caitlin rubbed her eyes with the heel of her free hand and pushed to a seated position. "What's up?" Her quilt fell off her shoulders, and she shuddered against the chill in the air. January had to be the longest month in Hunters Ridge, in the snowy region of Western New York. Cranking her heat would only be wasteful in this drafty old cabin. So Caitlin sucked it up, stacked her bed with quilts, and made a mad dash to the small space heater in her bathroom most mornings.

"Got a call about a disturbance in the area of 2 Bird's Nest and County. Just before you make your way up the ridge to that compound where those wacky so-called doomsday preppers are holed up." Wanda wasn't one to keep her opinions to herself, even as the sheriff tried to ease the town's concerns regarding the matter. There was probably a reason Wanda didn't show up at the town meeting today. The sheriff might have encouraged her to stay home for fear she'd speak her mind and rile up the Amish who were already unsettled. Caitlin still couldn't see what Wanda saw in Littlefield. The pair had been dating casually for years, much to Caitlin's disappointment. But who was Caitlin to ruin her friend's fun? She knew firsthand how hard it was to find a good man in town.

"Is it related to that group, or are you speculating?" Caitlin pivoted and sat up, giving herself a second to wake up.

"When do I speculate?" Wanda laughed, a popping sound deep in her chest that sent a trickle of fear fluttering across Caitlin's cool skin. *I can't lose Wanda, too.*

"Are you ever going to quit?" She knew it was futile to ask, but she had to keep trying.

"Life is about simple pleasures, my dear." Wanda grew serious again. "Got a call about a disturbance. Maybe someone breaking in. So get your butt in gear before the punks tear off into the woods." It wasn't unusual for bored teenagers to break into empty houses, something that wasn't exactly in short supply. Some seniors went south for the winter; other times kids just took advantage of vacant homes to party. Empty buildings—usually a little farther out of town—had also been used for meth labs. Her friend Olivia's sister-in-law had a gorgeous home on the escarpment that was unoccupied this time of year, but she kept it secured. And Caitlin took the occasional drive by to make sure it remained that way. Small towns didn't mean no crime. And lately Hunters Ridge had their share of it.

Her bedroom hardwood floor was cool to the touch as she rushed to the bathroom. She put the call on speaker and balanced it on the sink, hoping it didn't pick up the sounds as she quickly emptied her bladder and washed her hands, all while getting the pertinent details from Wanda.

"Who called it in?" Caitlin asked while buttoning up her pale blue deputy's uniform shirt.

"Wouldn't say. When I pressed for more information, I got the old 'I pay your taxes' bit and 'you better go do something about it.'"

Caitlin knew these kinds of people well. Entitled.

Demanding. Frustrating. Only the Amish required less from the department until lately. And their requests to save their sons came with a certain hesitation and a dose of humility.

Caitlin heard tapping over the speaker as Wanda entered something into her computer. "Town records show that address belongs to Richard Sanders." More typing. "Sanders died two years ago."

Caitlin sighed. "Okay, empty house. Maybe some kids are fooling around. I'll check it out." She grabbed her thick winter coat from the hook by the front door. "I'm headed out now. I'll let you know when I'm on scene."

"Want me to call Deputy Kimble? Maybe you shouldn't go out there alone." When Wanda wasn't giving her opinion about things, she was mothering Caitlin, one of only two female deputies in the Hunters Ridge Sheriff's Department. The woman had taken a special interest in Caitlin long before she had signed on as a deputy.

Caitlin clenched her jaw as she stuffed her gloves into her pockets. "Wanda, I'm a big girl. No need to pull him out of bed."

He probably wouldn't appreciate it since he was still technically honeymooning. He and Eve Reist had married in a beautiful ceremony just before Christmas.

Caitlin stepped outside and squinted against the falling snow. "Let me go, Wanda. Gotta clear the snow from the truck."

"Drive safely. Let me know when you're on location."

"Will do." Caitlin dropped her cell phone into her winter coat pocket and tugged on her gloves. She grunted as her boot sank into the snow-covered pathway. She glanced upward at the swirling snow. Were they calling for a storm? After a while, a person tuned out the cries of "snowmaggedon" from the broadcasters out of nearby Buffalo and Erie,

Pennsylvania, who enjoyed using scare tactics for a ratings boost.

Caitlin opened the driver's side door on her four-wheel drive, hopped in to start it up and cranked on the defroster full blast. Begrudgingly, she climbed back out and quickly swiped at the snow, watching it drop off her vehicle in big white sheets. "Next house is going to have a heated garage," she muttered to herself as she got back into her truck and put it in gear. The snow crunched under her tires as she easily made it out of her drive, only to turn onto icy streets.

Deputy Caitlin Flagler loved her job.

Just not on nights like this.

CHAPTER 4

Caitlin reached across the dash of her truck and grabbed the police radio. "Wanda, I just crossed County Road and I'm turning on Bird's Nest, approaching property on the left." The radio chirped as she removed her hand and waited for her friend in dispatch to acknowledge her. Wanda was probably the only other human awake at this ungodly hour.

"That's the one. Are you sure—"

Caitlin pressed the button on the radio, effectively cutting her off. "I'm pulling over on the side of the road. Driveway isn't clear. I'll be going up to the house on foot. I'm not seeing any tracks." If there were trespassers, they didn't come from this street. Not unless they came long before the storm. She squinted past her wipers moving against the rapidly falling snow. Didn't seem like much of a night to be breaking into a home, unless someone was trying to find shelter. "This is Sanders' house. Did the property change hands since he died?"

"Not sure. I'll look into it," Wanda said.

"Okay, I'm headed up." Caitlin got out of her truck and

found herself lifting her shoulders to her ears to stave off the cold. She squinted toward the home across the street. The yellow from a kerosene lamp glowed in one of the upstairs windows. Strange. Seemed not everyone was asleep at this hour. Maybe the anonymous call came from an Amish neighbor who had a forbidden phone. Caitlin made a mental note of it. Abram Troyer, who spoke out at the meeting, lived out this way. She'd have to check on that. Maybe he had a bone to pick with a newcomer. Despite their show of wanting to work as a community to make sure their sons weren't falling prey to the evil outsiders, the Amish didn't change much. They wanted to stay separate. So if they reported something, more times than not they did it anonymously.

Caitlin scanned the old Sanders' house. Everything looked still. Newly fallen snow tended to do that. A clean, white slate.

Deceiving.

Looking more closely, the indentations from earlier tire tracks were partially obscured by the rapidly accumulated snow. They disappeared up the driveway and behind a crudely constructed fence designed, by the looks of it, to keep out trespassers. Apparently someone had returned more recently. She looked back across the street. They had an unobstructed view of Sanders' property.

The fine hairs on the back of her neck prickled to life that had nothing to do with the weather.

Someone was watching her.

Caitlin had been in this line of work long enough to have a gut sense when something was up. Her mind drifted to Wanda's offer to call another deputy. Nope, wasn't happening. She had answered plenty of calls alone in the middle of the night. It didn't take two deputies to check out a vacant house, or worst case, chase some kids off the property.

Dipping her chin into her collar, she squinted toward the flurries that landed then melted on her eyelashes. If she were at home by a fireplace with a cup of hot cocoa staring out the window, she'd be inclined to say it was beautiful. Growing up in Western New York, she had seen her fair share of snowstorms and she loved them. When she wasn't out in one like a figure in one of those snow globes someone had turned upside down and shook. Vigorously.

Despite her warm leather gloves, Caitlin was able to unclasp her gun from her utility belt. Something was off out here. Something she couldn't quite put her finger on. On heightened alert, she took large, awkward steps in the snow, now at least twelve inches deep and counting. The crunch-squeak of her boots echoed in the night.

When she reached the crudely constructed gate across the driveway, she was surprised to see there was a people-sized opening. She grabbed her solid flashlight from her belt. The wind had created drifts in the snow, making it impossible to determine if someone had slipped onto the property, or if the wind had merely pushed it open. She flicked off the flashlight and let her eyes adjust to the darkness.

Vapor floated from her mouth on heavy breaths, and adrenaline coursed through her veins, making her forget the punishing winds. A few inches of new accumulation covered a full-size pickup truck that was parked around the back of the house, hidden from street view. She had far more snow on her SUV when she cleared it off tonight to respond to this call. Whoever was here had arrived sometime this evening. This wasn't an abandoned vehicle, or one previously used by the deceased homeowner.

She flicked on her flashlight. No obvious sign of forced entry or broken glass. She made her way around the entire house to make sure it was secure and had reached the truck again when a low voice growled at her.

"Get off my property."

Caitlin reflexively stepped back. The barrel of a hunting rifle was aimed directly at her. Her heart dropped. She ducked behind the truck and snagged her gun from its holster. Her years of training had kicked in. "Sheriff's deputy!" she announced. "Drop your weapon!"

CHAPTER 5

"Ah, hell." Austin lowered his rifle to his side as the flood of adrenaline slowly ebbed out of him. What in the world was she doing here? He had dozed off on the couch mid-chapter of his latest novel, only to be woken up by the crunching of snow underfoot. He hadn't come to attention that quickly since he had been stationed overseas on active duty and someone had breached their barracks. Thankfully, both times he had kept his boots, coat and gun by the door.

"Drop your weapon!" she hollered. He noticed a wobble in her voice, but he suspected it had more to do with the temperature than her nerves. Although he couldn't be sure. "Now!" she shouted when he didn't immediately comply.

"It's down." Austin relaxed his posture and set the rifle on the snow-covered ground, suspecting she wouldn't stop barking out commands until he complied. He held up his hands in a surrender gesture. He could have taken her, but he had no reason to risk a deputy's life. Or draw more attention to himself.

She stepped out from behind his pickup truck with her

gun still trained on him. He just wanted to go back inside. He despised the cold. He hadn't had a chance to zip up his coat in his hurry.

Austin adopted an annoying, cool swagger that came a little too naturally for someone who hated everything he was pretending to be. He took a step backward, away from his truck. If the deputy got a notion to search it, he'd be spending the night in lockup while they sorted things out. He didn't need that kind of complication.

"Don't move." The deputy aimed the obnoxious beam into his eyes. He shifted his hand to block the light, but squinted all the same.

"Want to get that out of my face?" Didn't she recognize him from earlier?

She gestured with her gun and flashlight moving in unison. "Name."

"Deputy, this is my property. There must be some misunderstanding." What had brought her out here? Had someone from the compound called in a report on him after seeing him drop off Elmer? Someone looking to harass him? His mind clicked through the possibilities as he tried to keep his jaw from shaking. *Man, it's cold.*

"This is Mr. Sanders' land." Her gun was aimed squarely on him, the accusation in her sharp tone unmistakable. "Do you have any other weapons on you?"

"No," he replied calmly, even as he wondered if there was a way to bring this young deputy into his confidence. No, it would take too long to assess if she was trustworthy. He couldn't risk her reporting back to the sheriff. "I'm renting this property from Sanders."

"Mr. Sanders is deceased."

"His daughter." He racked his brain for a minute, trying to come up with a name. If he had to stand out here for much longer, his brain wouldn't be the only thing frozen. Then it came to him. "Karen Sanders. She arranged it."

"What's your name?" she asked with the crisp efficiency of a deputy doing her job. Her watchful eyes glistened in the moonless night. She holstered her weapon and seemed to be debating something with herself. "Name?" she repeated. "And this time I am asking you for it."

Ah, she does recognize me from earlier. Maybe that was why she was holstering her gun, figuring he wasn't a complete stranger to Hunters Ridge. He had shown his face in town during daylight hours. But that was a stretch.

"Austin Young." He decided right then and there that he'd make her drag each piece of information out of him. He had nothing better to do. He certainly wasn't going to sleep. Adrenaline still coursed through his veins from his trip to the compound earlier. And now this unexpected guest. He gave her his date of birth because he knew she'd be asking for it.

"Do you have ID, Austin Young?" Her tone suggested she could probably give as much as she took.

The deputy relayed the information into her shoulder radio. He wasn't worried that she'd realize his ID was fake. He had been on numerous undercover assignments as an FBI agent, and his cover had to hold up for inquisitive bad guys.

"Do you have any documentation that you're renting here legally?" she asked. "It's not unheard of to have squatters around here. In vacant properties."

"Wallet's in the house."

She seemed to consider this for a moment. "What were you doing outside in the middle of the night in a storm?"

He cocked an eyebrow. "I suppose I could ask you the same thing." What he would do to rub a hand over his beard and shake off the snow. His entire body was going numb. He grew up in Buffalo, but first chance he had, he'd enlisted and got stationed south of the Mason-Dixon line. Didn't people from up here know that others lived with palm trees and ocean breezes?

"Got a report of a disturbance." In the heavy shadows he couldn't see her face, but he felt the intensity of her gaze. While he was in the army, he worked with powerful women like her. She was waiting him out. "Do you know anything about that?"

Austin considered it for a minute. Could he somehow work this in his favor? He'd have to be careful not to tip his hand to any of the parties. "I didn't call 911, if that's what you're asking."

"Why were you outside?"

"I heard you." Man, he was so good at playing this role that he was starting to annoy himself. "I don't like trespassers."

She jerked her chin toward the house. "Anyone else live here with you?"

"I live by myself."

"Which door is unlocked?"

"Neither. Not safe to leave your doors unlocked."

"Hunters Ridge is a pretty safe place."

"That's your opinion." He didn't know much about Hunters Ridge, but it seemed when Clyde Wheeler and friends set up camp someplace, the entire surrounding area got a lot less safe.

"Come on, let's get inside before you freeze," she said, her tone warming.

Austin wanted nothing more than to get out of the elements, toss a few logs in the wood-burning stove and throw himself on top of it. But he couldn't risk inviting a deputy into his home. "You're not going into my house."

"Stop being a tough guy. Let's get you inside where you can show me ID and your rental agreement, and I'll be on my way." She quickly glanced around. "Seems to me you might have a disgruntled neighbor."

Austin had a few brief conversations with Abram Troyer across the road. The man was rightfully concerned about the new guy in town, asking him if he was tied to the new group in town. Austin had been vague and dismissive. Maybe Troyer was upping his game to get some information.

"Come on," the deputy said, taking a step toward his house.

Austin debated arguing all the reasons he wasn't going to let law enforcement in. No real prepper would invite a deputy into his private sanctuary. He took another step and he couldn't feel his foot. *Dammit.*

"Either show me your ID now, or I'll take you down to the station to sort this out. We don't look kindly on squatters."

Austin was cold deep into his bones, and he was tired. "The second I produce my ID and lease, you'll leave?"

The deputy made a gesture, as if to say, *Cross my heart and hope to die.*

CHAPTER 6

Every inch of Caitlin's skin buzzed, and that was saying something because her hands were numb from the cold. Man, it was wicked tonight, and this guy was awfully skittish about letting her inside, which made her even more determined to see what he was hiding. He had no obligation to show her in, but if he willingly invited her in, she'd accept.

"Back door," Austin muttered.

She walked one step behind him, letting him tamp down the snow to make a path for her. Despite claiming the house was locked, the door wasn't. *What else is he lying about?* She focused on his every step, cautious about any sudden movements. He was a full foot taller than she and much broader. He could probably kick her legs out from under her and make a run for it. Once a drunk Amish kid elbowed her in the face, and he regretted it moments later when she introduced *his* face to the gravel on the side of the road. Caitlin hated drunks. Hated drunk drivers even more.

But if Mr. Young here decided to bolt, she'd probably let him go. Only a fool would want to remain outside longer than he had to in this weather. Soon enough, she'd discover if he was lying about renting this place from the deceased homeowner's daughter. It wasn't worth getting into a tussle over. Caitlin was confident Wanda was digging up more information on Austin Young since she had radioed in his name and date of birth a few minutes ago.

"Okay if I go in ahead of you?" His gruff voice floated on a stiff gust of wind.

"Go on." Caitlin reached out and grabbed the storm door as he pushed open the main door with a solid thwack of his shoulder. It seemed to get stuck in its frame like a lot of old houses.

Once inside, he palmed a light switch, casting the dated kitchen in a warm yellow glow. He stepped back, allowing her to enter. She studied his face. Something floated in the depths of his eyes that she couldn't quite read. Gone was the anger, replaced by something else. Amusement? The fine hairs on the back of her neck bristled to life, but she couldn't pinpoint the emotion: fear for her safety, or concern that this guy was getting to her in a way that few guys did?

You don't even know him. You only met him outside the fire hall. And now here. He could be an ax murderer come to town.

No, that wasn't the vibe.

Be professional.

Austin went to retrieve his ID. Caitlin kept the door in her peripheral vision as she scanned the counters and table. Nothing seemed out of place. There was a pile of mail and she slid the newspaper off it to see Mr. Sanders' name on an electric bill.

"Here." Caitlin spun around and found Austin standing in the doorway offering her his ID. She wondered how long he had been there.

She took it from him. "Military."

He nodded, a solemn expression on his face. "Retired. US Army."

Her eyebrows drew down. "When did you move here? I know most everyone in Hunters Ridge. I've never seen you around. Before yesterday."

"I like to mind my own business." His steady gaze went right through her. He didn't answer the question, and they both knew it. He jerked his chin toward the mail pile. "His daughter comes by once a month to collect the bills. Utilities are included in the rent." He fought with a narrow drawer and finally produced a handwritten document. "Here's our contract."

"Where do you work?" she asked. Surely someone his age had to have a job.

"You requested my ID and the rental agreement."

The steely look in his dark brown eyes made a flutter of unease coil up her spine. *What are you hiding?*

"So unless there's something else pertinent, I'd really like to call it a night."

"Just one thing." Caitlin squared her shoulders. She refused to be dismissed by anyone. "Any reason someone would send the sheriff's department out here in the middle of the night?"

"Nope." The single word held a cockiness that Caitlin was more than familiar with. It was the favorite response of many of the locals she questioned.

She considered the lonely light on in the house across the street when she first arrived. "Any trouble with your neighbors? Abram Troyer lives close by, doesn't he?"

Austin seemed taken aback. Or was it an act? "I'd be surprised if my neighbors knew I existed. They're Amish, I think."

"First time in a small town?" She raised her eyebrows. "Everyone knows what's going on at their neighbors'."

Austin shook his head. "Well, that may be true, but I don't know my neighbors. Like I said, I stick to myself."

"Are you familiar with Clyde Wheeler and the group he runs just up the way? You were at today's meeting at the fire hall." She watched him closely while she asked the question. Something flickered in the depths of his eyes before they returned to dark pools of nothingness. When he didn't answer, she angled her head and smiled, taunting him, "You look like the kind of guy who might be—"

"Involved with a doomsday preppers group?" His question held an air of disbelief.

"Are you?"

"Small town. I hear things. Doesn't mean I'm part of it." Again, he didn't answer the question. His posture sagged a bit, and he ran his hand over his beard and struck a conciliatory tone. "Of course I know about the group."

"True enough," Caitlin said, still struggling to get a read on this guy. "Anything the sheriff's department should be aware of?"

Austin leaned back on the counter and crossed his arms. "It's late. You saw my ID."

"I suppose you won't tell me what brought you to Hunters Ridge?" Caitlin pressed.

"I'm tired."

Caitlin reached into her coat pocket and pulled out a business card and set it down on top of the pile of mail. "In case you think of something."

Austin picked it up. "Caitlin Flagler." He raised his eyebrows. "Nice to meet you." His tone suggested it was a casual meeting and rubbed her the wrong way.

"Deputy Flagler," she corrected him.

"Good night, deputy." He stared at her until she had no choice but to turn and leave. He was who he said he was. At least his ID matched his story.

She sensed his gaze boring through her as she trudged through the snow to her SUV parked on the dark country road. She groaned when she saw that more had accumulated on the windshield. She climbed in, cranked the engine and put the front and rear defrost on high.

She called Wanda over the radio. "All clear over on 2 Bird's Nest."

"It might be clear now…" The dispatcher said with the air of someone who had a secret.

"What is it?" Caitlin twisted the wiper control knob and watched with a strange sense of satisfaction as the heavy snow slipped off the front windshield.

"I did some digging on Austin Young."

Caitlin slumped in her seat and tugged off her damp winter hat. Her mind flashed back to the gun aimed at her. He was ready and waiting for something, or someone. She cleared her throat. "Any arrests?"

"No, but his name popped up on an internal report."

Expectation charged the air as she waited for Wanda's big reveal.

"Austin Young paid for Elmer Graber's bail."

A sinking feeling settled in her gut. "When Elmer was arrested for DUI in December? Why would he do that?"

"Why indeed?" Wanda almost sounded gleeful. She lived for town gossip.

Caitlin reached up and pulled the seat belt across her and clicked it into place. She cranked the heat up to high and paused, staring through the swirling snow at the old farmhouse.

What are you up to, Austin Young?

CHAPTER 7

The next morning the sun rose bright, creating shimmering diamonds on the freshly fallen snow. This was the kind of day Austin woke up to as a kid in Buffalo and flipped on the TV to see if his school was closed. Then he'd spend the entire day playing outside. Now he only went out in the elements if he had to. Lately, it turned out to be more than he cared to.

Austin stomped his feet to remove the snow from his thick winter boots. The sales guy at the big-box sporting goods store wasn't kidding when he said they'd keep his feet warm. He did a quick check on the gun safe behind a false wall in the barn. Then he checked the one locked in his trunk. Everything seemed in place.

These weren't just any guns. They were his ticket into the compound.

Back inside the old farmhouse, Austin slid off his green scarf and draped it over a peg near the door. He could imagine a black felt hat hanging on that same peg and wondered what they would think about an ungodly man like him living here. According to Karen Sanders, her father had grown up Amish but stopped following the rules after his parents died. He remained in the family home and later met and married a woman outside his faith. Turned out the next generation of Sanders had veered further from their Amish ancestors. Now their daughter was a pharmaceutical sales rep living in the suburbs of Buffalo who inherited a house she didn't have time to clear out and sell.

Austin could relate to the amount of energy it took to close up a family home after his parents' deaths. He shook his head, dismissing the thoughts that crowded in on him. He filled up the old silver teakettle. If only his concerns were that straightforward. He flicked on the knob to the stove and listened as it hissed a fraction of a second before the gas ignited into a steady flame. Instant coffee wasn't the best, but it would give him the caffeine jolt he needed. He rubbed his hands together as he waited for the kettle to whistle. He stared out over the snowy landscape and worried that as everyone settled in for the long months of January and February, his efforts to infiltrate the compound would be slowed. As it was, the holidays had cost him time. Wheeler had apparently left to visit family. And a nagging dread suggested that if he didn't find a way in quick, he might never.

An intermittent buzzing noise drew his attention to his phone sitting on the small kitchen table. When he saw the name of the incoming caller, he froze, hand hovering over the screen. He'd prefer to give her a positive report, but this morning he wasn't feeling especially positive.

Realizing that she'd never stop calling until she got ahold of him, Austin picked up the call. Tear off the bandage in one fell swoop. "Hey, Janelle," he said, his voice gravelly first thing in the morning.

"Hi, Austin," she whispered, as if she didn't want anyone to overhear. Perhaps she was at her mother's house, next door to the home where he grew up. Or maybe her small children were having their breakfast within earshot. Could that have been his life if he had made different choices? He had been so eager to get out of Buffalo, away from what he thought was his parents' "small" life.

"I saw Hunters Ridge got a lot of snow," she said, as if warming up to the purpose of her call.

"Did the snow bands miss you guys?"

"Yes, we got just a few inches, but most fell south of the city." As it often did.

Austin's skin grew itchy. He wasn't much for small talk. "I don't have any new information about your brother."

"No?" He could almost see the hope deflate from her. Janelle's younger brother's disappearance had taken a toll on Janelle and her mother. Janelle had once been head cheerleader in high school, graduated valedictorian, and gone away to a top university. They had dated on and off since they were sixteen, and had finally decided they were better friends than dating material in their mid-twenties, much to the consternation of both of their families who thought they were destined for one another. But Austin had seen another world in the Middle East, and Janelle had seen new horizons after finishing her graduate degree. Their relationship had been destined to fizzle out. Neither of them had seemed heartbroken. Funny how things worked out.

Perhaps the one person most devastated had been Janelle's younger brother, Christopher, who might have taken Austin's deployments too personally. He had looked up to Austin, like an older brother. And Austin had let him down.

Austin turned off the burner under the kettle and poured the steaming hot liquid over the instant coffee grounds. "Progress has been slow, but I'm not giving up," he said, forcing a bit more optimism into the words than he felt. He was a lone wolf out here and even if he finally gained access to the compound, it didn't mean he'd immediately have answers. He had to gain their trust. That wasn't going to be easy.

He imagined Janelle with the Sunday paper spread across the kitchen table, tapping the eraser end of the pencil on the crossword puzzle. He never had the patience. She cleared her throat. "You've always been a sweet guy, Austin, telling me what I need to hear. What my mother needs to hear. But what's the truth? I didn't mean for you to make this your life's work." There was a sadness to her tone. Perhaps guilt for getting him involved. But what choice did they have?

Austin took a sip of his coffee and grimaced, wondering why he hadn't picked up a real coffeepot and grounds. Seemed like a problem for another day. "This group is up to something, but they're very protective. I hope to gain access soon. Find Chris."

Janelle's younger brother had come home excited about a preppers group he had joined in Hunters Ridge. He had alluded to them growing some "pretty fine weed," and it was no big deal because local law enforcement didn't care. Janelle had been unable to pry more information out of him. She didn't worry too much, considering marijuana was legal in some states, but a short while after Chris returned to Hunters Ridge, he went radio silent. Janelle had tried to get answers herself from the compound and then the sheriff but everyone seemed to close ranks. The only information the compound shared with her was that he'd left on his own. Now, Austin was investigating, a task made more difficult because he didn't know who to trust.

"Be safe." Janelle's voice cracked. "Chris wouldn't run away and not tell my mother. That's not like him. He's had his share of problems, but he loves our mom too much."

"I always thought of Chris like a little brother." Eight

years his junior, the kid used to ask to tag along when his big sister and Austin went for ice cream or hiking, or other family-friendly dates. And it was Austin's enlisting that had the most influence over Chris, who enlisted many years after him.

A familiar guilt crowded him. Unfortunately, when Chris returned, he wasn't the same person. He seemed to be searching for the sense of brotherhood he had found in the military. Perhaps that was what he sought in Wheeler's group.

But where was he now?

With the heavy weight of responsibility, Austin was determined to uncover the truth. No matter what it took.

CHAPTER 8

Caitlin sat with her coffee in her cozy kitchen overlooking her snow-covered yard. The plow service had been here sometime between when she finally fell asleep after her middle of the night visit to Austin Young and when she woke up at six a.m. No matter how tired she was, she could never sleep past this early hour, even on her days off.

She forced herself to linger over breakfast for as long as she could. Her therapist said she needed to find peace in doing nothing. Caitlin was new to therapy after growing up as the only daughter in a strict religious family that put more stock in prayer than talk therapy. It didn't help that her mother commanded her obedience, yet turned around and lived a life of excess. Perhaps she had been afraid her daughter would become like her, but didn't have what it took to turn her own life around. Caitlin drew in a deep breath, trying to quiet the obsessive thoughts that tried to fill every still moment.

Find peace.

But she had a feeling that wouldn't come easily today.

Caitlin drank the last of her coffee. Fueled with caffeine, she pushed back from the kitchen table and set her dishes in the sink. She grabbed her laptop from on top of the piles on her dining room table and brought it into the kitchen. She found Wanda's email that had been sent in the early morning hours and clicked on the attachment.

She squinted at the form Wanda had scanned in, trying to make sense of the messy handwriting. Her heart started racing and a mix of disappointment and curiosity pumped in her veins as she read the documentation that proved Austin Young had bailed Elmer Graber out of jail. Why would someone who claimed to be new to town, and didn't know a soul, pay for a local Amish kid to get out of jail after crashing his buggy under the influence? Especially a kid who was prone to getting in trouble with the law.

She'd grabbed her cell phone to call Wanda to ask her what else she knew when the time made her pause. Just because Caitlin worked all night and got out of bed at the crack of dawn didn't mean everyone did.

Caitlin flipped closed the laptop and smiled to herself. Wanda might not be up, but the Amish were. *Man, I really need a hobby.*

Caitlin got dressed—she'd wait to shower—and stuffed her wild bed-head hair into her winter cap, got bundled into her thick coat, and headed out. She'd make this visit as a civilian. Her breath came out in vapor that hung in the air momentarily before dropping onto the freshly fallen snow that glistened like diamonds in the early morning sun.

Something about this Austin guy niggled at her. And someone else—whoever called the sheriff's department to report a disturbance at his quiet property—also seemed to have him in their sights. Why? Who was he messing with? His proximity to the preppers' compound and his appearance at the town meeting couldn't be a coincidence. Could they? And why would Austin Young pay Elmer Graber's bail? Nothing made sense, but she'd figure it out. She was sure of that.

However, she'd have to play her visits to the Grabers' farm cool. The sheriff didn't like his deputies to rile up the Amish, and if he found out she was doing it on her day off *and* a Sunday, he'd probably demote her to desk duty. That big conditional was *if* he found out. She had no plans on letting him know. Besides—she further rationalized her argument—the Amish didn't like to talk to law enforcement, especially this particular Amish person, leaving her no option but to show up while she was off duty.

What she did on her time was her business.

Once in her SUV, it took less than ten minutes for Caitlin to reach the Grabers' pig farm. She was pretty sure this was an off-Sunday, meaning no service, and the Amish would only do the necessary chores and spend the rest of the day with family. Next to the Grabers' was the Reists' residence. Only a few months ago, Dylan Kimble, a fellow deputy, had to clean up a slaughtered pig on his now-wife's doorstep. It had been meant to intimidate the former Amish woman into silence, but it had only spurred her to fight back against those who were harassing her. They hadn't been able to pin that bloody mess on Elmer, but if Caitlin had extra money to throw away, she'd bet it on the tough Amish kid who had long ago lost his way. Maybe while she was questioning him, she could ask him about this. She had a strong dislike for bullies. Any man her mother had brought into their lives was a bully. Ruling by intimidation.

Caitlin parked her truck on the road out of respect for the Amish. She trudged up the unplowed lane on foot. She could hear a scraping noise coming from the barn, so she headed in that direction. As she got closer, she flung her arm and buried her nose in the crook of her thick coat sleeve as her stomach revolted. She could not imagine what the pig farm would smell like in warmer months.

Caitlin paused about twenty feet from the opening and called out, "Elmer Graber!"

The pigs squealed in response. Somewhere not too far off a rooster crowed. A shadow moved in the barn and a chill raced up Caitlin's spine and her fingers twitched. She had a gun strapped to her ankle, but she didn't want to spook Elmer. She already had a precarious relationship with him. In past encounters, she never let him forget who was boss, something he didn't take kindly to. She forced her shoulders to relax.

Go in easy. She was just here to talk. Get him to open up.

"What do you want?" a gruff voice barked out from inside the barn. Caitlin tilted her head and realized it was Mr. Graber, Elmer's father.

"Morning, sir," Caitlin said, trying to smooth the look of disgust that she suspected was on her scrunched-up face. "I'm looking for Elmer."

The elder Graber regarded her for a moment. "What's he done now?" He jabbed his pitchfork into the hay and stepped out of the barn. His broad-brimmed hat fell short of covering his red-tipped ears.

"Nothing new that I'm aware of." Caitlin wanted to placate the man.

"Then I suppose you have no business out here." The dirty, packed snow squeaked under the heels of his well-worn boots as he trudged past her, back toward the main house. "Have some respect for the Sabbath."

"I wouldn't ordinarily come here on a Sunday…" She took

a step forward and her boot sank into the snow. "It's important."

He slowly turned. Something flashed in the depths of his eyes that she couldn't quite make out. The shame and anger when an adult child didn't follow the tenets of the Amish was a heavy burden. She didn't want to cause this man more pain, but she needed to know the connection between Austin Young and his son. Because she knew there was one.

"He's not here," Mr. Graber repeated. "You won't be talking to him today."

"Do you know where I could find him?" She yanked off a glove and hooked a strand of hair that escaped her hat and had stuck to her lip.

Mr. Graber jerked his chin, his beard, in no particular direction. "He's taken up with those newcomers."

Caitlin's heart raced. And the stranger from last night just might be involved with those same people. "The group that's taken over the old Hershberger farm?"

"*Yah*. That's the one."

She considered her next question carefully. "Do you know how he became connected with them?" She suspected the same way Clyde Wheeler had lured other young Amish men to his compound, but she wanted to hear it from him.

"They're hiring for construction. Honest work for honest pay." Mr. Graber bowed his head and gave it a subtle shake, as if trying to understand how something seemingly innocent had gone wrong.

Or maybe she was reading too much into it. She had no idea if the work was anything but ethical. Her heart went out to the man all the same. Elmer wasn't the only child Mr. Graber had "lost." His oldest daughter, Abby, had left the Hunters Ridge community to work at a gorgeous country home on the escarpment, close to the compound. Abby had followed her employer to New York City, where she was murdered. It was a tragedy that had a ripple effect on this poor Amish family and the community at large. Caitlin wasn't unfamiliar with loss, but the loss of a child was incomparable to any other.

Mr. Graber met her gaze. "He started coming home with ideas I couldn't get behind. The final straw was him playing target practice with a high-powered rifle with a few of my pigs." Crystals formed on his beard from the condensation of his breath. "Those pigs are my livelihood. We raise them and sell them. We treat them humanely." His harsh tone left no room for interpretation. He was disgusted with his son.

"Does Elmer live at the compound now?"

Mr. Graber reached down and snatched an overturned bucket half buried in the snow. He set it on a makeshift plywood roof over a pen for some unseen animals. Perhaps he had moved them all into the barn during the storm. "*Neh*. He sleeps here. Most nights." He cleared the emotion from his throat. "My son didn't come home last night, but I pray he has a change of heart. It's past time he was baptized and settled down. But he makes one bad choice after another."

Caitlin nodded. "I'm sorry for your troubles." She paused a moment. "I have one other question, and I promise I'll be on my way."

Mr. Graber lifted his gaze to hers and sighed. He was a man with the weight of the world on his shoulders.

"Did Elmer ever bring any of the outsiders here? Or perhaps mention a new associate by name?"

Mr. Graber shook his head. "*Neh*, I don't know anything about his business there. All I can tell you is whatever they're doing is ungodly. I'm afraid the devil got hold of him a long time ago."

"Why do you say that?"

The older gentleman furrowed his brow. "How do you suppose that man is paying all these Amish boys?"

Caitlin's heart raced. "Do you know something, sir?"

Mr. Graber waved his hand. "Perhaps I've said too much."

Caitlin knew when to cut her losses. "I'll let you get back to your work." She smiled tightly.

Mr. Graber scoffed and picked up the metal bucket, then set it down again, as if remembering he was on his way to the main house. "There's enough work on this farm for five men, and my only son…" His voice trailed off and she couldn't make out the rest of whatever he was muttering, but she understood the sentiment. Completely.

CHAPTER 9

After leaving the Grabers' farm, Caitlin checked the clock on her dash and calculated that Wanda would be up by now, having a cigarette with coffee and her tuna sandwich while binge-watching something on Netflix. Years ago, when Caitlin arrived at the house after school, it was soap operas that captured the woman's attention. Caitlin smiled to herself, wondering if the soaps were still on in the afternoons. And if they were, would she recognize the characters that never seemed to age over the decades? She'd probably never know because she rarely turned the TV on during the day, but like most people, she enjoyed streaming shows at night when she was too tired to focus on a book.

A few minutes later, she pulled up the long lane to Wanda's quaint house. She knocked on the door quietly and went right in, as per usual. She hated that Wanda never locked her door, but Caitlin had stopped hounding her about it. The older woman claimed two things: they lived in a small town, and why would someone want to bother with an old lady?

This from the person who worked dispatch at the sheriff's department. She knew exactly what went on in Hunters Ridge. Or maybe she counted on the gun she kept in the drawer next to the couch, and a second one in her bedroom nightstand.

"Hey Wanda!" Caitlin called as she followed the sound of the television into the small sunroom that had been converted into a four-season room, but it still felt drafty to Caitlin. Perhaps it was the panoramic view of snow all around them. She lifted her hand with the box of Timbits. "I brought donut holes."

Wanda waved absentmindedly, a cigarette burning between two tar-stained fingers. Her friend was dressed in her favorite jeans and a sweater that highlighted the blue in her eyes. She was usually in sweats and sweatshirt on a Sunday morning. Neither of them were the churchgoing type. Caitlin was immediately suspicious, but kept her thoughts to herself. She averted her gaze from a gory scene—apparently, Wanda was finally binge-watching *Dexter*.

The credits came on and the next episode cued up. Wanda pointed the remote at the screen and paused it. "You see this one?"

"A few episodes." The violence made her uneasy. She had to deal with enough mayhem in her day-to-day work life. When she relaxed, she preferred tamer fare.

Caitlin hoisted the box of donuts again, eliciting a smile from Wanda this time. "You were always my favorite." The woman took the box and peeked in, inhaling. "Thank you." She set it down and pushed some magazines off the couch cushion next to her. "Did you get the email I sent?" She kept her voice hushed.

"Yeah."

"I found that very curious, didn't you?"

"I did. Nothing else on Austin Young?"

"No." Wanda picked up the box and pulled out a donut, her eyes growing round. She said, "I really shouldn't" before taking a big bite. She swallowed the mouthful. "Dinner tonight? I was thinking we could order Mexican food."

"Olivia invited me over for dinner. I'm sorry." Caitlin unzipped her coat as she sat down on the couch. "Want to come with me? I'm sure she'd love to see you."

Wanda waved her hand. "No, I've got my heart set on takeout. Thanks, though." She put the donut down and wiped her fingers on an old, crumpled napkin.

Caitlin rubbed her chapped lips together. She dug into her pocket and pulled out some ChapStick. There was never a tube far from reach. She applied the balm and considered this. "Any thoughts on why this Austin guy might have paid Elmer's bail?" Her mind kept circling back to this.

Wanda shrugged. "Nice guy, maybe?" She tore off a piece of the donut and popped it into her mouth. "Do you know where he's originally from?" she asked around the donut. She lifted her hand to block the puff of white powder that sprayed from her mouth.

Caitlin slowly shook her head and laughed. "Good donut?"

"Sorry about that." Wanda smiled in return.

"I have to think there's some connection to the preppers' compound. Right? Guy's new to town. Elusive as all get out. Helps an Amish kid who's tied to the group? Shows up at the meeting yesterday."

"How do you know Elmer's involved with them?" Wanda wiped her mouth with the back of her hand.

"I just came from their farm. His father told me he's spending a lot of time up there. That can't be a coincidence, right?"

"What can't be a coincidence?"

Caitlin shifted in her seat to find Sheriff Littlefield standing in the doorway. A flush of heat washed over Caitlin. She hadn't realized anyone else was here. Why hadn't Wanda given her a heads-up? Maybe because they both knew she probably would have scooted out before she was forced to make small talk with her boss, a man she cared little for.

Caitlin pushed to her feet and shook her head. "I didn't realize you had company." She bit back another apology. She was trying not to apologize for things she had no reason to be sorry for.

Wanda reached out and tugged on Caitlin's hand. "Sit down. Finish what you were saying. We just got back from breakfast a little while ago. Jimmy was checking the sump pump in the basement. I'm worried about the flooding when all this snow melts."

Feeling a bit like she had been telling stories outside school, Caitlin shook her head. "We can talk later." The sheriff wouldn't take kindly to her running her own investigation.

"Don't let me interrupt," the sheriff said. Something flashed in the depths of his eyes that made icy dread pool in her belly.

She felt foolish for talking freely with Wanda, but why would she think they had an eavesdropper? And that was what he had been doing. She felt it in her bones. She hadn't heard him coming up the basement stairs or opening the door. But why did it make her so uneasy? If he had been listening and had an opinion, wouldn't he share it? And why hadn't she noticed his vehicle? Had he parked it in the garage or on the street?

"I really should be going." Caitlin waved her hands in no particular direction. She hated that she was babbling like a schoolgirl in front of the sheriff. Then to Wanda, "See you on Tuesday. Maybe I can bring Chinese food."

"Make sure you get egg rolls." Wanda smiled, seemingly unaware of—or ignoring—Caitlin's discomfort.

"I always do." Caitlin made her tone sound light even as her heart was racing in her chest.

CHAPTER 10

*L*ater that day, Caitlin leaned over and rocked the bouncy chair holding her godchild, Charlotte Kincaid, who didn't look like she had a care in the world as she held her tiny fist to her mouth and blew bubbles. "Hello there. Aren't you the cutest thing?"

The baby's mother, Olivia, shut off the kitchen faucet and dried her hands on a red and green dish towel, apparently part of the decorations—including the small tree in the corner—that had been left over from Christmas a few weeks ago. "You know, you can pick Charlotte up. She won't break."

Caitlin sat back and frowned. As an only child, she didn't have much experience with babies. "What do they say, 'let sleeping babies lie'?"

"I think that might be dogs." Olivia shrugged. "And she's awake. But whatever."

Caitlin smiled at Olivia's subtle mocking of her. The two women had become fast friends over five years ago when they both joined the sheriff's department at the same time. They were—then and now—the only women in the department, as if the plan to be more diverse was complete and they could go back to their regularly scheduled programming. Sheriff Littlefield always projected an air of annoyance, as if he had done them both a huge favor. Now she felt the need to prove him wrong.

Ah, such was life in a small town, or perhaps that of a woman who had grown up without a father figure. And she had watched her mother seek approval in men. The wrong kind of men. At least Caitlin had enough sense to avoid making bad choices about men in her life.

Inwardly, she laughed. There were no men in her life. Not of the dating variety.

The rich aroma of lasagna reached Caitlin's nose, and she turned her attention to her rumbling stomach. She missed her friend's camaraderie at work, like a security blanket. Without her, Caitlin felt a little unmoored. Or perhaps it was her randomly running into that stranger yesterday. Not once. But twice. She thought about asking her friend if she knew anything about him, but decided against it. How would Olivia know him? She'd been hunkered down with her beautiful baby for the past few months. Besides, her well-meaning friend would latch onto her query and never let it die. Girlfriends, *best* girlfriends, were allowed to do this.

So, instead, Caitlin asked, "Any thoughts on when you'll come back to work?" Looking down at the sweet baby's face, and even though Caitlin suspected she lacked the maternal gene, she had enough empathy to understand leaving this little one in someone else's care would be difficult.

Olivia threaded the dish towel through the oven handle. "Ah, you miss me," she said in a singsong voice as she slid into the kitchen chair next to Caitlin's and gazed dreamily at her baby.

"It is nice to not be the only female deputy around."

"Well…" Olivia looked up at her with reservation in her

eyes. "I asked the boss for an extension. At least until Charlotte is a year old."

Ah, so her earlier claims of "re-evaluating in the spring" were meant to be a way of putting off telling me this disappointing news.

"Oh." Caitlin couldn't help but feel a little defeated, but then she quickly caught herself. This wasn't about her. "I mean, that's great. I'll definitely miss you, though." Perhaps that had been the reason she had been invited for dinner, to soften the blow of Olivia's announcement. But did it really come as a surprise? Wouldn't she do the same thing if the situation were reversed? *Doesn't a mother owe it to her daughter to be there for her?* A hint of regret—loss—whispered through her. Did anyone ever survive the loss of a parent? The baby shifted in her bouncy seat and blinked open her pretty blue eyes. Upon seeing her mommy, she smiled and a saliva bubble formed on her pink lips. The dark thoughts from Caitlin's own childhood immediately slinked back into the recesses of her mind. Who couldn't feel lightness and joy while looking into that beautiful face?

"I can barely make it through the day as it is with the limited sleep because of this cutie. Right, you know that?" Olivia playfully shook her daughter's pink crocheted slipper. "This one still likes to eat around the clock."

Caitlin couldn't imagine being responsible for someone who was completely dependent on her.

"I'm sure you'll manage just fine without me."

Caitlin rolled her eyes. "I'll try."

"Seems the town is in an uproar about the preppers group compound." Olivia unbuckled the baby and changed the subject. She lifted her daughter into her arms, sending a waft of baby shampoo and laundry detergent into the air, mixing with the savory dinner smells.

"I was surprised to see you at the meeting," Caitlin said.

Olivia kissed Charlotte's plump cheek, and the baby

cooed. "I was curious." She cut her friend a sideways glance. "Aren't you?"

"Of course I am."

Olivia nestled the baby against her and caressed her tiny face. "Any idea what might have really happened to the Amish boy? The sheriff has written it off as a hunting accident."

"You don't believe that?" Caitlin studied Olivia as she bounced and cooed in her daughter's ear, soothing the child. Not only was she a fantastic mother, but Olivia was a great deputy. She had a talent for reading people. She had been a key member of the group that had tracked down a stalker a few years ago who had become obsessed with a young Amish girl in the community. Caitlin shuddered at the thought of something happening to her friend. Funny that she didn't have the same worry about herself.

"Well, if I wasn't on leave, I'd probably want to talk to the Miller family. Get a sense of who the dead Amish boy was. How involved had he really been in the compound? Was he a big hunter?" Olivia lifted a knowing eyebrow. "I overheard some people at the fire hall saying that Aaron wasn't much for the sport. I would have inserted myself in the conversation, but Charlotte picked that exact time to let out a wail."

"Interesting. A while back, Sheriff Littlefield said to leave the family alone. That they were in mourning."

"Never do the hard work when it's easier to do nothing." Olivia shrugged. "Drew sees a lot of these guys at the lumberyard because of the construction on the compound. That's for sure. I don't know if they're up to no good, but they've been good for business."

Caitlin wasn't sure she wanted to get into her gut feelings that there was something illegal going on up there. Mr. Graber alluded to it. Or maybe it was just because she couldn't understand the need to hunker down like the end of the world was around the corner. She needed to do some Google searches for what drove those groups. "I don't know about Aaron Miller, but I have discovered that Elmer Graber has been up at the compound."

"Doesn't surprise me. That kid's been trouble since day one."

Elmer had been arrested for harassing Violet Cooper, now Olivia's sister-in-law. He got off with a slap on the wrist only to be picked up for drunk driving more recently. She was convinced he was behind an unsettling scene where someone slaughtered a pig and left it on his neighbor's porch with a threatening message. If there was some way she could tie Elmer to something that would stick, she'd love to see him spend some time in jail before he really hurt someone with his reckless choices.

"Caitlin?"

She looked up and, based on the expression on her good friend's face, she realized Olivia must have called her name a few times. Without asking her to repeat herself, Caitlin added, "I still think he got away with killing that pig and leaving it on Eve Reist's doorstep last fall. The word 'sinner' was written on her door in blood." Eve had grown up Amish, left to work in Buffalo, and was home visiting her sick mother at the time. For the sake of her family, or so Eve claimed, she didn't want to press charges. That part of her job was maddening. Caitlin wasn't near as forgiving as the Amish.

"You can't fault Eve for wanting to move on with things. Her relationship with her family was already strained. She's former Amish married to a sheriff's deputy."

Caitlin sighed. "That's the biggest frustration. How do you enforce laws when the Amish want to live separately? Or don't want to stir the pot once they've left." This wasn't a new complaint in Hunters Ridge, but Elmer Graber's flaunting of the rules was really getting under her skin.

Olivia held out the baby. "Can you hold Charlotte while I finish setting the table?"

"I'll set it." Caitlin made to stand up, and Olivia placed her hand on her knee.

"I'd rather you held your goddaughter." The new mother smiled, and Caitlin had no choice but to take Charlotte. "Just support her head." Olivia gently settled the baby in the crook of Caitlin's arm and leaned back, as if assessing the situation. "Look at you! A natural."

Caitlin adjusted her arms, tenderly tucking in one flailing arm under the cozy blanket. "I'm not sure I'd say I was a natural, but oh my...what a beautiful baby." She smiled at the child's precious face, and deep down she detected what she suspected might be a maternal stirring. Who knew?

"She takes after her mother." Olivia laughed as she opened the cabinet and grabbed some dishes. "Now, other than work, what have you been up to?"

"Your mommy thinks I have a life outside of work," Caitlin said in a singsong voice directed toward the baby. "You've got it made, kid. Hanging out in your bouncy chair and having people carry you around." Charlotte stared right back and Caitlin couldn't help but smile. The baby cooed and her entire face lit up. "Hey! She smiled at me!" Olivia laughed while she finished setting the table with four large plates.

"Wait, who's the fourth plate for?" Olivia had never mentioned one of the grandparents or other friends coming over. Heat flooded her cheeks. "Who's coming to dinner?" she repeated, trying to keep her voice even, despite suspecting her friend—forever the matchmaker—was up to something. The last time she had attempted it, it had ended in disaster. Olivia had made the mistake of trying to set her up with a tough-guy sort who didn't take kindly to Caitlin being a sheriff's deputy. She wasn't sure how her friend made such a big swing and a miss on that one.

Olivia smiled in that easy way she had. "It's just someone Drew met at the lumberyard. They have a lot in common as retired army. Thought it might be nice to have a little get-together."

Caitlin suddenly had the urge to bolt, but baby Charlotte tucked comfortably in her arms prevented her from moving. Her friend had planned it that way. Olivia knew Caitlin was held captive while holding Charlotte.

Olivia blinked rapidly with puppy dog eyes, in an exaggerated attempt at pure innocence, any signs of uncertainty gone. "I thought it would be fun to mix it up a bit."

"Mix it up or set me up?" A flush of heat washed over Caitlin. She swallowed hard, then readjusted the blanket over the baby's arms. Why was she getting so flustered? It was just dinner.

Male voices sounded from the mudroom, and Caitlin sucked in a breath. It *was* only dinner. Olivia's eyes opened wide, and she lunged toward Caitlin. "Here, give me Charlotte," she whispered. "I don't want him to think you're already taken." Then she laughed at her own joke, and Caitlin couldn't help but laugh too.

"I'm going to get you for this," she whispered harshly as she leaned forward in her seated position and handed over the baby. She immediately missed the warmth of the little body in her arms. Or maybe she thought the baby would serve as armor for whatever lame night this might turn out to be. Despite herself, she pushed to her feet and smoothed her palm over her shirt, now wrinkled from holding the warm bundle. Wrinkles or not, she wasn't exactly dressed for making a strong first impression. Her jeans and T-shirt with hoodie were meant for errands and a casual dinner with friends. Nothing more.

"You look fine," Olivia whispered, reading her friend's mind, as she often did, swaying back and forth with a suddenly fussing baby. "Who knows? Maybe you'll thank me." Olivia took a step closer and spoke so no one else could hear. "Don't be so quick to judge. Maybe he's the one."

"Stop!" Caitlin hissed but couldn't help but laugh at her predicament. She couldn't very well be rude. What could one dinner hurt with a stranger she'd never—hopefully—have to see again?

Drew entered the room first. Their guest followed. Caitlin's eyes locked with the man's and her traitorous heart exploded. Drew turned to introduce them. "This is my wife Olivia, and her friend Caitlin."

"Nice to meet you," Olivia said, offering a free hand while holding the baby in the other arm.

"'Lo," Caitlin squeaked out as she flicked him a feeble wave. *Oh man, what am I doing?*

"And this is my friend, Austin Young."

CHAPTER 11

"Hello," Austin said, having to quickly check himself when he saw Deputy Caitlin Flagler. "Nice to see you again." He hadn't expected to meet her here. He had to admit it was a pleasant surprise, but based on her flushed cheeks, she didn't share in his take on events.

Austin handed his heavy coat to Drew and then bent to undo the laces of his snow boots in the mudroom off the kitchen and recalibrated his expectations for the night. His host, Drew, had met him at the door with the usual commentary about if he had trouble finding the place and how the snowy weather didn't make it any easier.

"Your directions were perfect." Besides, Austin had already scoped the place out. He had been looking for a way to get close to someone in the sheriff's department. To determine what Chris meant when he said the sheriff didn't seem to care what was going on at the compound. Was it not worth caring about? Shooting guns and getting high? Or was there something far more nefarious happening?

Austin smiled. "It's good to meet a few more people when you're new in town." He hadn't anticipated having dinner with two deputies. Maybe—finally—his plan was coming together. If he could get Deputy Flagler to buy into his story. After last night's events, she'd certainly be skeptical of him.

The smell of a home-cooked dinner reached his nose, and his stomach growled. A pang of guilt for using these people nudged at him. He didn't have a choice. He had to get answers.

"I bet you're not used to this kind of snow, coming from down south," Drew said, interrupting his thoughts.

"Well, I was stationed down there, but I'm originally from Buffalo," he said, careful to sprinkle his cover story with bits of the truth. Just like the truth about being retired army. That tidbit had led to a connection with Drew in the lumberyard, and then this dinner invite. Score one for the workings of a small town. All he had to do was throw out a few details about his bachelor life and not knowing anyone. It was presumptuous on his part that he'd score an invitation, but it'd worked. Getting close to Drew—the husband of a deputy—was easier than trying to buddy up to someone from the sheriff's department directly, especially since Elmer revealed Drew was married to a deputy, which made him squirrelly about going to the lumberyard. Working his way into the compound was taking a long and circuitous route of tips and manipulation.

"Where are you staying?" Olivia asked.

"A place on Bird's Nest." Austin's gaze drifted to Caitlin's, and he forced a nonchalant smile. Based on the narrowing of her pretty blue eyes, he had achieved the effect he was going for. The aloof loner who moved into a cabin in the middle of winter. He had a role to play.

"You said you had an uncle who left you a place? What's the name?" Drew asked. "I'm relatively new to town, but my wife probably knows him."

Stick as close to the truth as you can. He hadn't followed his own advice.

A niggling started in the back of his brain and his attention drifted to Caitlin, who had taken a seat at the kitchen table and was studying him. He hadn't counted on having a run-in with her last night. He'd have to tweak his story. "Actually, I rented the place I'm staying in from the daughter of Mr. Sanders."

"Aww, poor Dick. They'd call him Old Man Sanders." Drew glanced at his wife, not mentioning the fictitious uncle again, thank goodness. "I guess I have been around this town long enough to get to know some of the residents." Then to Austin: "If I recall, he was working on projects in that house right until he got sick. God rest his soul."

Drew's beautiful bride seemed to take on a walk-bounce-walk-bounce cadence that Austin had seen in other new moms as they soothed their babies. "Come on in. Don't let my husband leave you standing there." She held out her hand to the chair next to Caitlin's at the table. "Have a seat."

Austin hesitated. "Wow, you didn't say you had a newborn." Now he felt a little bad about securing an invitation for dinner.

"No worries," Drew's wife said with a bright smile. "We're happy to have you. Drew tells me you were stationed at the same base."

"Yeah, yeah. But we never overlapped." Austin had done a Google search to get some of the basics and hoped at the same time that wouldn't be much of a topic of discussion. "I've been out a while. I stayed down south for a bit, bouncing between Georgia and Florida—can't beat the weather—and now I'm here."

"Why here?" Caitlin asked, suspicion sharpening her tone.

The million-dollar question. He had a prepared answer.

He slid his fingers into the back pockets of his jeans, assuming a casual gesture. "Just wanted to get away."

Drew's wife must have sensed Caitlin was about to pepper him with questions because she held up her hand. "This is our daughter, Charlotte." She handed the baby over to her husband.

Austin didn't know much about babies, but he did know you should say something agreeable. "Beautiful."

"Do you have kids?" Olivia asked as she pointed at the seat next to Caitlin again. The house was warm and cozy. A gas fireplace flickered on the back wall of the large eat-in kitchen.

Drew reflexively held up his hands. "Oh, no. Not me." Then realizing his faux paus, he added, "I mean, I hope to someday. When I meet the right person." Aww man, Austin had entered the cliché version of the person he was pretending to be. But was he really pretending? Wouldn't he love to have a beautiful wife, a baby, the stability of a family?

Olivia laughed. "Trust me, this guy was all thumbs when it came to Charlotte. Now he hardly lets me hold her when he's home." She tipped her head toward the kitchen table. "Dinner is almost ready." Austin lingered at the back of the chair. Olivia must have sensed the vibe because she said, "Have you two met?"

"We have," Caitlin said, then to him, "I hadn't realized you were such a social guy." She seemed to catch herself and she added with more than a touch of sarcasm, "Nice to see you again."

"How did you meet?" Olivia persisted.

This was his chance. "It's a funny story, really," Austin said, like it was all some silly, bizarre misunderstanding.

Caitlin leaned back and crossed her arms over her chest, as if to say, *I can't wait to hear this.*

"Deputy Flagler here—"

"Caitlin, please," she interrupted, her tone droll.

"Caitlin"—he eyed her warily— "responded to a call last night at my place. Someone reported a disturbance, but the only disturbance was me having to roll out of bed in the middle of the night in a snowstorm because of a sheriff's deputy in my yard."

"Wow, really?" Drew said, gently rubbing his daughter's back, eliciting a burp. "Small world."

Caitlin watched him with a steely gaze. Not exactly the trusting type. And rightfully so. She pointed to Olivia. "We're both sheriff's deputies. But I imagine you knew that." An air of suspicion weighted her words. "And you just happened to befriend Drew at the lumberyard." He felt three sets of eyes studying him. Four if he counted the baby in Drew's arms.

"Lots of projects at the cabin."

"That you're renting?" More suspicion. "Not from your uncle." She gave a knowing tilt of her head. "Why work on a place you don't even own?"

"You'll have to excuse my friend," Olivia interrupted. "She's focused on that group—that preppers group—not far from where you're staying." As soon as the words left her mouth, her law enforcement instincts apparently kicked in and her cheeks colored. "Are you friends with those people?"

Drew touched his wife's arm.

"I've met a few of them in town." Austin rubbed his beard. "But like I told Dep—Caitlin," he quickly corrected himself, "I like to stick to myself. Mostly." He shrugged, doing his best to look sheepish. "I'm hard-pressed to turn down a home-cooked meal, though."

"Well then, let's sit down." Olivia set a tray of lasagna on the counter and Drew put the baby in some chair thingy on the floor.

Austin sat down. He could feel Caitlin's eyes boring into

the side of his head as he pretended to take great interest in Olivia and Drew putting the rest of the food on the table.

"So, Austin, you grew up in Buffalo. I went to the university there," Olivia said as she put a large piece of lasagna on his plate. "I didn't live far from the south campus," she offered. "Came back to Hunters Ridge to work in law enforcement. They were looking for women." Olivia jerked her thumb toward her friend. "Caitlin grew up in Hunters Ridge. Her family settled here before the Amish arrived."

Ah, there was a safe topic.

"I don't know much about the Amish. They seem like a fascinating people," Austin said. "I imagine they're a tourist draw in the summer."

"Oh yes," Olivia said, "the traffic on Main Street on Saturdays when they set up the farmers market is unbelievable. I mean, for a small town. You'll have to check it out."

"I will," he said noncommittally.

"Do you have plans to stick around till summer?" Caitlin asked, scrutinizing him.

"I might," he said.

"You might," she muttered.

"I'm sorry, did I do something to offend you?" Austin asked.

Caitlin sat up straighter, then shot a furtive glance over to her friend, then to Drew and the baby. She relaxed her posture almost as quickly as she had gotten fired up. Apparently she had reconsidered, perhaps realizing she had been too abrasive. She forced a cheery smile. "Nope, just like to know a little bit about the newest resident of Hunters Ridge."

CHAPTER 12

Caitlin tracked Austin as he stood up and carried his plate over to the sink. She didn't care if she was being obvious about it. What was this guy up to? How did he know Elmer Graber, and why was he suddenly buddy-buddy with her friends? She had managed to be polite during dinner, but she didn't want him to leave without answering a few questions.

"Fantastic dinner. Thank you," he said. "It's been a long time since I've had a home-cooked meal."

"You're very welcome," Olivia said as she reached over and fussed with Charlotte's blanket on the bouncy chair.

"I should call it a night. I'm sure you have to get the baby settled," Austin said.

Caitlin was about to ask him how he knew Elmer, when Drew's chair scraping across the floor caught her attention. She shot him an angry look that slid off her face when he smiled and said to Austin, "Stay for dessert. I made pumpkin pie." Drew, God love him, enjoyed baking. Caitlin narrowed her gaze at Austin. Doubt he baked in his rented log home in his spare time.

She swallowed the question about Elmer.

Austin held up his hand. "No, I should go. Thank you for your hospitality."

Caitlin's pulse beat in her ears. A part of her felt as if she had been incredibly rude. Yet her gut told her this man was up to no good. She sat rooted in place as Drew escorted Austin to the back door. He returned a few minutes later and scooped up the baby who had started to fuss and said, "I'll give Charlotte her bottle so you ladies can visit." He paused, patting his precious daughter slung over his shoulder. "Leave the dishes. I'll get them after I put the baby to bed." He kissed their daughter loudly on the cheek and winked at Caitlin.

"He's a showoff, isn't he?" Caitlin said. Her friend had landed a winner—or a talented actor.

"Thanks," Olivia said to her husband, ignoring her friend's jab. Olivia picked up her plate, kissed her husband, then set it in the sink. Caitlin followed suit.

Olivia filled up the sink with hot soapy water, apparently letting her hubby off the hook. She paused and leaned her hip on the counter. "What was that all about? Did something happen when you responded to that disturbance call out at Austin's place the other night?"

Caitlin slid the dishrag off the oven handle and twisted it. Biting her bottom lip, she stared off after Olivia's husband. "I don't know." She rubbed the back of her neck, trying to ease the knot. "Doesn't it seem odd that he befriended Drew? Like maybe he's after something?"

Olivia picked up a plate and set it in the water. She grabbed a dishcloth from the drawer and turned slowly, as if considering. "I don't see it." She shrugged. "Maybe I have new-baby brain, but he seems like a nice guy. New to the area. Looking to make a few connections." Olivia scrubbed the plate in slow circles, then rinsed it with warm water. She handed it to Caitlin, who dried it.

She considered that for a moment. "Maybe." She glanced out the window over the sink, but all she could see was her own reflection. Something about this felt all wrong. She dried the next dish and stacked it.

"What's on your mind?" Olivia coaxed.

"Remember how Elmer Graber got arrested for DUI last month?" She waited a beat before continuing. "Well, your new friend bailed him out of jail. And earlier today I went up to the Grabers' farm—"

"Oh, Caitlin…" Olivia knew her friend's heart. There was no love lost between her and Elmer.

Her best friend's pity made her stomach knot. "It's not…" It was her turn to stop talking.

"Elmer will get his due. It's not solely your responsibility to see to that." Olivia turned the water off and led Caitlin over to the table with a damp hand to her friend's elbow. "You can't make this personal."

"How can I not?" The prickle of tears at the back of her eyes came as a surprise. She thought she was tougher than this. "Drunk drivers ruin lives."

Olivia drew Caitlin's hands into hers. "Your mother's death was tragic. Do your job, but don't make it personal."

Caitlin pulled her hands away. "I don't want anyone else to go through what I went through." She let out a slow breath. "Drunk drivers make me so mad." Her heart was racing in her throat. Nights like this—a cozy family night—made her miss something she never had.

Olivia nodded. "I know, sweetie. I know." She tilted her head and smiled. "As law enforcement officers, we need to get every drunk driver off the road. Just don't allow it to consume you."

Caitlin swallowed around a lump in her throat.

Olivia pulled out a kitchen chair and held out her hand in invitation. "Would you like some wine?"

Caitlin let out a long breath and sighed. "No, thank you. I'd probably fall asleep."

"Tea, then." Without waiting for an answer, her friend made a couple cups of tea and they settled in at the table. Olivia took a sip. "Tell me why Austin is ruffling your feathers?"

Caitlin pulled the tea bag out of her teacup, wrapped the string around the spoon, draining the amber liquid, then balanced them on the edge of the saucer. She missed having her friend at work to bounce ideas off of. "Mr. Graber told me Elmer was tied up with the compound and now I learn Austin bailed Elmer out of jail."

"Is that illegal?" They both turned to see Drew standing in the doorway. He jabbed his thumb in the direction of the baby's bedroom. "Charlotte's out like a light."

Olivia stood. "Thanks, sweetie. I'm going to check on her." They brushed hands as she passed, and a twinge for what Caitlin was missing made her heart ache.

Drew came fully into the kitchen and leaned back on the counter. "Austin seems like a sincere guy. Even if he is tied up with the compound, they're just a bunch of people who are trying to be self-sufficient. Considering the world we live in, that can't be all bad."

"No, I suppose not. But Clyde Wheeler is recruiting a lot of young Amish men, and upsetting the community."

"Is that any different than when they run off for Buffalo or other areas and otherwise leave the Amish? At least this way, they're not far."

She studied Drew. She always respected her best friend's husband, but she couldn't be as trusting as he was in this stranger. "I have a bad feeling about this preppers group." She used air quotes over the last two words and slid to the edge of her chair. "Aaron Miller had started working at the compound shortly before he ended up dead."

"In a hunting accident, right?" Drew held up his hands.

"Did he say anything more about what brought him to Hunters Ridge?" She tried to remember what they had previously discussed. He had seemed less standoffish today than he had when she rolled up to his place in the middle of the night. But an all-out interrogation over lasagna would have been rude.

"He was looking to get away." Drew bowed his head and rubbed the back of his neck. "Look, I was in the army and felt pretty lost when I came to Hunters Ridge. If I hadn't met Olivia, hadn't been given the job by her brother at the lumberyard, I might be inclined to join a group like this, too. Sometimes people just have a need to belong."

"But a survivalists' group?"

"They're growing in popularity."

Olivia appeared in the doorway and smiled. "Ah, to sleep the sleep of babies," she said around a yawn.

Caitlin sighed heavily. "If only." She stood and turned on the water again. "Let me help you finish the dishes."

Drew gently touched her shoulder. "I've got it."

She smiled at her friend's husband. "You really are too good to be true."

"I'm blessed, that's for sure," Olivia said.

Caitlin turned off the water. "Just be careful who you let into my goddaughter's life."

"I'd never let anything happen to them." He gently squeezed her elbow. "I'm a good judge of people, too."

I hope so.

CHAPTER 13

The walls of Austin's drafty farmhouse grew close. He didn't get how Old Man Sanders had lived out his days in the dark place. The thick curtains pulled over the few windows. He supposed the heavy fabric was a stopgap measure to keep out the cool air, but the deep shadows and damp smell made the house feel uninviting. Austin made a strong cup of coffee and went outside to sit on the rocker on the front porch. The sun was rising over the tall pine trees. Austin had learned a long time ago that there was no weather too cold, not if a person dressed for it. He had spent a good chunk of his teenage years skiing in Ellicottville before enlisting and moving south. As his dad used to say, "You can put more clothes on when it's cold, but you can't take off more when it's hot out."

His breath came out on a vapor, and after the backs of his thighs grew numb from the cold from the wood seeping through his jeans he settled in. He had been too lazy to put on his ski pants.

He took a long sip of his coffee and thought about his exchange with Caitlin Flagler last night. Apparently they were destined to keep running into each other. She was one fiery pistol, and she seemed to have it out for him. If that was the case, she was a solid judge of character. He wasn't who he claimed to be. Not entirely. She probably sensed that. He couldn't help but wonder if the job had made her that way, or if she had come into it that way. He took another sip and stared at the glittery snow.

His plans weren't going as expected. He had hoped to get more information on Sheriff Littlefield by getting close to Drew and his deputy wife. But he hadn't counted on Deputy Flagler showing up again. She seemed to have a knack for doing that. He wondered what she knew about the compound, and her boss.

Austin had been in Hunters Ridge for six weeks on his own, slowly making connections to the compound. His most solid link was Elmer, and he was proving to be the focus of Caitlin's attention. Maybe he had made a miscalculation in getting close to the Amish rebel. But beggars couldn't be choosers.

Maybe, just maybe, he could pull Caitlin into his confidence.

"I will not let you down, Chris. Not again," he muttered to the winter wonderland. The longer he holed up alone out here, the more he found himself talking out loud to himself. To the kid he considered a little brother. Maybe this was the way of life out in the country where acres of snow and ice separated him from his neighbors. He hadn't met any since he moved in, but that was okay with him. He'd noticed the horse and buggy going in and out across the way, but the one time he tried to approach them, the man of the house waved him away. Austin didn't need to be asked twice. He suspected this man was the one who called the sheriff's department on him. Perhaps he had grown tired of hearing target practice, the one activity Elmer and he shared. The kid couldn't seem to get enough of his guns. Now, Austin had floated out that he was going to come into possession of a high-powered rifle. He couldn't risk losing the kid's attention.

This country lifestyle was unfamiliar to him. Growing up in Buffalo, the wintery landscape involved helping neighbors dig out their cars to move to alternate sides of the street. In the summer, his parents' house was so close to his neighbors he could hear Janelle and her little brother arguing. Austin didn't mind the privacy country living afforded, but it didn't help him gain access to the compound. His first break was when he'd heard rumblings at the bar that Elmer had been arrested for DUI. He took it upon himself to pay his bail. Ingratiate himself to the kid. It seemed to be working.

The deep rumble of a faulty exhaust system had him leaning forward. *Speak of the devil.* The icy snow crunched under the smooth rails of the rocker. A familiar orange clunker appeared at the end of his lane, and he suddenly remembered his offer of target practice.

Austin stayed seated. Elmer Graber climbed out of the car and followed the tracks made by the tires of Austin's truck. He had planned to plow it out as soon as the caffeine hit his veins. But now he didn't need the coffee to be on high alert. This kid was his ticket into the compound. He felt it deep in his bones.

Elmer lumbered up the long driveway, a shotgun in his hand and a goofy smile on his face. A subtle unease tickled the back of Austin's throat, the same internal alarm system that kept him alive on each of his deployments. And on his assignments with the FBI. But this felt different. Elmer was a piece of work, but deep down he didn't believe this kid was a threat. Not to him. Not yet. He was too naive. The poor kid had left the Amish but hadn't invested in a decent haircut, seemingly content with the bowl cut and patchy beard. Suddenly self-aware, Austin ran a hand across his own bushy beard. He, at least, took clippers to the sides of his head to keep himself from looking too shaggy. It was time he had another trim.

In a FaceTime call, Janelle had told him the facial hair suited him. That lots of women dug the lumberjack look. Not her, of course. She had settled down and married and lived the stable life that a military man turned FBI agent couldn't provide her. Yet they had remained friendly.

Elmer raised his shotgun in a nonthreatening manner. "How's it going?"

Austin slowly stood and set his coffee mug down on the glass side table that probably should have been brought in with the first frost. He braced himself on the railing and scanned the road. His latest arrival seemed to be alone. "You're up early."

Elmer planted his hand on his knit hat. "Lifetime of living on a farm puts your body in a rhythm it can't shake." He jerked his chin in his direction. "What's your excuse?"

"Don't get to sleep in when you live in a war zone." Again, truth in his cover story.

Something flashed in the depths of the young man's eyes that Austin couldn't quite decipher. Fascination? Disgust? Intrigue? He had read somewhere that the Amish were conscientious objectors. But this one didn't seem to follow the Amish rules, and he undoubtedly had a propensity for firearms.

"Thought maybe we could do some target practice."

Austin scratched his eyebrow, trying to act nonchalant. "Yeah, um, sure." He picked up his mug from the glass table and reached for the door. "I'll be right back."

Austin left Elmer outside—he didn't want to let him know where he kept the high-powered rifle that had drawn him here. He was taking a tremendous risk letting someone from the compound know he had access to such weapons, but this was the only way in. He had tried for weeks with no luck to get a job in construction up there. Too many Amish men for that. Guns were his last big play. He just had to control the way things went down.

No more deaths would be on his conscience.

Austin rushed down to the basement, yet another location for his stash. *Don't put all your eggs in one basket.* He could see the lower half of Elmer through the cloudy windows, partially obscured by snow. He appeared to be pacing. In the deep shadows, Austin turned the tumbler and the door of the safe opened with a quiet whoosh. He glanced over his shoulder to make sure—however unlikely—that Elmer wasn't peering in. Austin removed the case with the semiautomatic from the safe and closed it.

Austin stepped out onto the porch and set the black case on the glass table. He zipped his coat up to his chin, trying to act casual. He had dealt with his share of bad guys in his life, but he'd had his troops or his fellow agents behind him. Now he was acting completely of his own accord. He gestured with his head. "I have some targets set up behind the barn. If the snow hasn't buried them." He laughed ruefully.

"Gotta practice in all weather. You never know. You have to be ready," Elmer said, following him.

His platitudes made Austin think of the YouTube videos of doomsday preppers he had been watching. His indoctrination. That, and some FBI files he had access to. This particular group hadn't been on their radar. "Ready for what?" Austin asked casually.

"For civil war. This country is divided." Over his shoulder Austin could see the tight set of the kid's mouth. "The collapse of our government."

"Wouldn't you have better luck remaining separate if you stayed among the Amish?" Austin slowed and turned around, the black case of his weapon banging against his leg.

Elmer twisted his face. "The Amish are sitting ducks. Once the established structures break down, desperate people are going to flee the cities and seek refuge in the country. With their farms, canning, self-sufficiency, they'll be prime for the picking."

"And the compound is prepared to fight back." Austin studied the man's face.

"Yes, sir." Elmer set his gun down on a clear hay bale that had been shielded from the storm by the run-down barn. "We will defend the property."

"That's why you need these weapons? To fend off outsiders when everything goes sideways?"

Elmer seemed to back down a bit. "We have to be prepared."

Austin set down the case and flicked the lock and the lid flipped open. He held out his open palm. "All yours."

The kid's covetous eyes sparkled as he stroked the weapon. "Seriously?"

"Go for it." Austin slid on a pair of headphones and stood back while Elmer took tremendous delight in shooting up a hay bale with a target painted on it. Austin's fingers twitched until he had the gun safely back in his possession.

"That's sweet," Elmer said, seeming more Buffalo teen than Amish outlaw.

"It sure is." If his neighbor was annoyed with him before, he'd be especially annoyed now. Without asking if the kid was done firing the weapon, Austin secured it in its case and told Elmer he'd be right back. He returned the weapon to the basement safe.

Back outside, he found Elmer on the phone in front of the barn with his head dipped in serious conversation. Austin debated backtracking, giving the kid time to talk, but Elmer looked up and met his eye, effectively forcing Austin to continue his approach. The Amish kid smiled brightly, revealing crooked teeth, stained from too much coffee and tobacco. A cigarette was dangling from his free hand.

Elmer ended the call. "Are you interested in coming up to the compound?"

Austin's scalp prickled. *Play it cool.* "Yeah, but I've got lots of work to do around here. Maybe another time?"

"Clyde Wheeler wants to see you now."

Austin drew his brow down, feigning confusion. "What's the rush?"

"You want to meet him or what?" Elmer picked up the rifle he had arrived with and hugged it to himself with a self-satisfied you-know-what-eating grin. "He wants to meet you now." Elmer narrowed his gaze, suddenly growing curious. "You said you're looking to make some money, right?"

Austin had carefully planted every detail with the kid, slowly over weeks at the bar so as not to raise anyone's suspicions. Had his plan finally made some inroads into the elusive preppers' community?

"Always looking to make some cash." Austin nodded, his heart thudding in his chest. "Does he need more construction workers?"

Elmer shook his head. "Grab your gun. Wheeler wants to make you an offer."

CHAPTER 14

Caitlin spent her lunch break at Wanda's. She drove up her friend's plowed driveway and parked alongside the house. Wanda hired out all these tasks. She hated the winter. She claimed she was moving to Florida as soon as she retired, which Caitlin speculated wasn't anytime soon. Truth be told, Caitlin feared that day. Wanda was the closest thing she had to family.

Caitlin called out to Wanda as she walked right into the woman's cozy house, just like she had done since the summer after high school. She had been eighteen—technically an adult—but she was forever thankful Wanda stepped in after her mother's sudden death. Dismissing the thought of that tragic event that was never far from the forefront of her mind, Caitlin opened the fridge and studied the contents. She could hear the noon news floating in from the sunroom where Wanda kept the TV.

"There's some chicken salad in the container on the top shelf," Wanda hollered by way of a greeting. They had an easy camaraderie that, if Caitlin was being honest, she feared would be altered if Wanda and the sheriff ever got married.

As it was, they maintained separate residences, and the sheriff's teenaged children from a previous marriage kept him busy. Besides, Wanda had claimed the sheriff had too many financial responsibilities, and she wasn't about to jeopardize her comfortable retirement, "thank you very much."

Caitlin smiled and slid out the container. "You hungry?" she asked as she unwound the twist tie from the one hundred percent whole wheat bread she had turned the older woman on to. She supposed it was all futile as long as her friend kept up her pack-a-day habit.

"No," Wanda hollered back, "I just ate breakfast." Sure enough, a small pan with crusted eggs on its edges soaked in the sink. The woman kept an irregular schedule the days following her twelve-hour night shifts, something she did three nights a week.

Caitlin plated the sandwich, shook some salt and vinegar chips out, and grabbed tonic water from a case sitting on the counter. She carried it into the sunroom where she found Wanda kicked back in her recliner, a snuffed-out cigarette in the ashtray on the table next to her. Caitlin lifted the plate. "Thanks for lunch."

"Anytime." And she meant that. Wanda kept Caitlin's favorites stocked. Some might see it as a small gesture, but Caitlin would never take it for granted. Not after the childhood she had with a mother who didn't always remember she had a daughter to care for.

She set her plate down on the coffee table. "You alone?"

Wanda shot her a look that said, *What do you think?*

While undoing her utility belt so she could sit comfortably, Caitlin shrugged. She set her belt with her gun on the couch next to her. She wolfed down the sandwich. "You make the best chicken salad."

Wanda pointed the remote at the TV and turned it down. "It always tastes better when someone else makes it." She set the control down on the arm of the recliner and twisted to face her. "Do you have any photos of the baby?" Her friend made a grabby gesture with her fingers.

Caitlin smiled and snagged her cell phone out of the case on her utility belt and scrolled through a few photos that Olivia had taken of her holding the baby.

Wanda looked up, beaming. "Look at you. A natural."

"That's what Olivia said." Caitlin rolled her eyes. "Just because I'm approaching thirty doesn't mean I need to be in a rush to have babies." Normalcy, yes. Babies, not so much.

"Gotta meet a guy first," Wanda deadpanned.

"That, too. And it's not like there are any guys whom I haven't already met in this Podunk town." Austin Young's handsome face floated to mind. Yeah, not exactly the kind of guy a sheriff's deputy should date. His reputation alone would tank her career. "Speaking of which, Olivia invited some guy over for dinner. She was trying to set us up."

"Really? Who would that be? You already know everyone in town."

"Remember that disturbance call the other night?"

"On Bird's Nest Road?"

"Yeah. Austin Young. The guy who paid for Elmer Graber's bail."

"He's that good-looking, huh?" Wanda asked, a spark of humor brightening her eyes.

"Wait, don't get sidetracked."

Wanda waggled her eyebrows, totally enjoying this.

Caitlin narrowed her gaze. "There's something suspect going on. I stopped by the Grabers, and Mr. Graber said Elmer was up at the compound. I think Austin's involved, too."

Wanda held up her palms. "Flat out ask him."

Caitlin's face heated as if she had been scolded, then she

let out a long sigh. "I didn't want to tip my hand. I need to secretly figure out what he's up to."

"How does Olivia know him?"

"Drew met him at the lumberyard. Both have a military background. Drew doesn't actually *know him*, know him, but—"

"I get it. They share the brotherhood. Not a bad thing."

"Something about him rubs me the wrong way." Caitlin leaned back on the lumpy couch.

"You're too picky." Wanda snagged the remote and turned the channel to some game show rerun and clicked the sound up a few notches. Caitlin kept her mouth closed while the contestant answered a few simple questions without missing a beat.

"Wouldn't it be nice if life had a lifeline?" Caitlin asked.

Wanda didn't peel her eyes from the TV. "Isn't that what I am?"

"Okay, I'd like to use a lifeline," Caitlin said, standing up and wrapping her utility belt around her waist. "Tell me why Elmer Graber is hanging out at the preppers' compound and Austin Young is helping out Elmer. So, by my logic, the new man in town is tied to the compound."

"Is there a question in there?"

Caitlin was deep in thought, trying to snap the pieces into place.

"Nothing wrong with living out in the country and keeping to yourself." Wanda tilted her head. "We do live among an entire group of people that like to stay separate."

"Aren't you curious what goes on at the compound?" Caitlin stuffed her arms into her jacket and zipped it up. "I watched some films about those groups on YouTube. They attract rugged, outdoorsy folks."

Wanda shrugged. She had seen a lot of eccentric during her lifetime as a dispatcher.

Caitlin flipped up her collar. "Well, I better get back on patrol." She stood and slipped her utility belt on. "Still up for takeout tomorrow night?" They had a routine, but this was their usual goodbye: making plans for their next get-together.

Wanda nodded, then she dragged a hand through her hair. "What does he look like?" A hint of humor laced her tone.

Caitlin quirked her head, as if she didn't understand the question, then she gave it up. They both knew Wanda was talking about Austin and would keep pestering her until she answered. "Dark hair. Beard. Lumberjack vibe." She tried to sound nonchalant. What she left out was piercing brown eyes, broad chest, big hands. The things that wouldn't go on a Wanted poster.

"Not the tough-guy type." Wanda laughed quietly, calling her bluff. Then she grew somber. "I've been paying attention to the calls coming in. There's no evidence of anything illegal up there. Lots of truck traffic going in and out, but no reason not to think it's construction supplies." She shrugged as if to say, *What do I know.* "I'm just dispatch."

"You're the ears of the operation."

"Jim knows Wheeler. He's stopped over once or twice when we were watching a movie." Wanda shrugged, as if that legitimized whatever was going on up there. "Didn't stay long. Wheeler seemed friendly enough."

"What did he want with the sheriff?" Caitlin asked, her curiosity piqued.

"Jim said Wheeler had some questions about adding security to their compound." Wanda frowned. "Who am I to judge? The people who feel they need to prepare for the end of the world might be a little different, but that doesn't mean they're doing anything wrong. Goodness knows, sometimes it feels like the world has gone off the rails." She adjusted the plush blanket over her lap. "Take a drive to the compound. Mr. Graber said Elmer was up there, right? Go find him. Claim it's a welfare check per the family." She sniffed. "Just make sure you're not making this personal."

Caitlin was about to protest when Wanda held up her hand to stop her. Caitlin's dislike of Elmer hadn't been a secret. She struggled to deal with drunks after growing up with one.

"I'm going to take a nap. I have another long shift tonight."

Caitlin picked up her plate. "Thanks for lunch."

"Anytime." Wanda yawned. "Be careful on the roads. They're calling for more snow."

Caitlin laughed. "What's new?"

Wanda closed her eyes and Caitlin thought she was drifting off to sleep, but before Caitlin made it to the kitchen doorway, she heard the woman mutter, "Apparently, a tall, dark and handsome man with a beard."

Shaking her head, Caitlin slipped out the side door. She prayed her dear friend didn't move to warmer weather. Caitlin would really miss her.

CHAPTER 15

Austin's fingers twitched as he sat in the passenger side of Elmer's car. It smelled of rancid fast food and feet. But that wasn't what made him uneasy—it was the lack of control sitting shotgun in someone else's vehicle, approaching a location he wasn't familiar with. But he had painstakingly laid the groundwork for this exact moment and couldn't retreat now.

Austin squinted toward the expansive tree line climbing up the ridge. The bare branches marked the slate sky. More snow was on the way. He just hoped they were back home by then. As it was, Elmer's bald tires fishtailed whenever they met a patch of snow or ice on each curve of the road. Austin didn't want to end up in a ditch somewhere. He worried this old clunker would fold onto itself, leaving them trapped and mangled. He tugged on his seat belt, reminding himself he had been in far more precarious situations in an armored vehicle in war-torn countries. If he could survive—by the grace of God—land mines and sharpshooters, he could navigate his way through some men who feared the collapse of society as they knew it. He had to get close enough to figure out what happened to his former girlfriend's little brother. He hadn't risked showing Chris's photo to Elmer for fear of revealing motives other than making a quick buck by trafficking guns. He had to play this just right.

He had to play that especially cool, too. A person didn't approach a person offering guns for fear of setting off major red flags.

"Mr. Wheeler doesn't meet with people that often," Elmer said with the excitement of someone who has been trying to catch someone's attention. Like a lost son eager to return to the father's fold. "When I told him about your high-powered rifle, he wanted to see it."

Play it cool.

"Yeah, these things are hard to come by." Austin took on an air of indifference. There was no way he'd hand over serious firepower to a man, an organization, with questionable motives. A feeling of unease gathered at the back of his neck and he tried to shake it off. He had to be on his A game. "I don't want to draw any heat."

Elmer shot him a smug look. He opened his mouth, then seemed to think better of it. The young man's beard had grown in patchy. Pink blossomed on his pimply skin. "I thought you were looking to get on the compound."

"For construction work." Austin kept his tone even. Guns were his backup plan, and it was working like he had hoped.

"He's got plenty of Amish men for that." Elmer drummed his fingers on the steering wheel to some beat in his head. "You told me you knew how to get whatever you needed."

"That's what I told you." With the hopes he'd go running to Wheeler. *Play it cool.* "I mean, if he really needed something, I'd have to see what I could get my hands on." Austin watched Elmer under the auspices of staring out the driver's side window. "Might be expensive."

Worry? Concern? Distrust? Maybe a mix of all three

flashed on Elmer's face. Then, just as quick as that, it was gone. The Amish kid slanted him a hard look. "Whatever you do, don't promise him something you can't deliver." He lowered his voice, as if someone might overhear. An ominous warning. "He's got a temper. Real mean temper." Austin suspected the kid was regretting getting involved with this transaction, yet he seemed eager to please.

"Hmmm..." A niggling started in the back of his head and he found himself holding his breath, waiting for Elmer to give him more information. But Elmer really wasn't the chatty type. It had taken Austin weeks to draw the kid in. To dazzle him with promises of target practice with powerful guns after it seemed gaining access to the compound by offering his construction skills was going nowhere. He had to work as many angles as he could. To find Chris. He tamped down the guilt sloshing in his gut. Elmer was eager to please, and if it meant Austin had to use him, so be it. Elmer would look good in the old man's eyes. Win-win.

Unless something bad had happened to Chris. Then all bets were off. Justice would be served. A new thread of unease wound up his spine. He'd have to figure out how to deal with his supervisor if and when that time came. He just hoped he wasn't about to torpedo his three-year career with the FBI since he had decided to act on his own under the guise of taking a leave to handle his deceased mother's estate. He scrubbed his hand across his face. *Worry about that later. Get your head in the game.*

"That man smells BS a mile away," Elmer said in a somber tone. "We'll show him the weapon." He shot him a sideways glance and raised his eyebrows. "If he wants more, you can get more, right?"

"I'll try." Austin stifled a smile. Poor kid. Totally lacking in self-awareness. He'd gone from his Amish home to the influence of a doomsday preppers group.

The first hints of a headache crawled across Austin's temples. The acrid exhaust and frigid winter air seeped through a thin crack in the floorboard, offering a glimpse of the racing asphalt under his feet. The last thing he'd planned to do was not play it cool. After weeks of acting like a loner in Hunters Ridge, he got a wayward Amish kid to give him an introduction to the compound on Hunters Ridge, the last known location of Chris Rutherford. There was no other way in because he couldn't trust the sheriff's department. Janelle Rutherford had run into a brick wall after her meeting with Littlefield. So that meant the sheriff was lazy and didn't want to do his job, or that the sheriff was crooked and was protecting whatever was going on up there. Chris had alluded to as much. Austin got the same vibe at the town meeting: the sheriff didn't want any feathers ruffled, namely the ones of the stocky man running the compound on Hunters Ridge.

"How long have you known Clyde Wheeler?" Austin jerked his chin in the general direction they were headed. The man was wary of new people. So how did Elmer get in?

Elmer slanted him a suspicious glance. "You've never asked me about this before."

"I was never on my way to meet him. Who made the introduction for you?" Austin shrugged casually. "He's obviously a very careful man."

Elmer let out a long breath and scrubbed a hand over his face. He seemed to puff out his chest, apparently taking pride in his position as a go-between. "Some of the guys I worked with at the cheese factory were doing construction for him."

"They recruited you?" Austin already knew the answer; he had been doing a lot of intel on the sly.

"You could say that. Some of them stuck around. Others went back to the factory or their farms." Elmer scratched his head roughly through his black knit winter cap. "I suppose it's not for everyone." That was probably the most insightful thing the kid had ever said.

Austin remained quiet, waiting to see if the kid would keep talking. He didn't have to wait long.

"Clyde pays us pretty well. He's adding onto the main house. Elmer made a sucking noise with his lips against his teeth. "I thought the Amish liked to be self-reliant, but these guys are obsessive." Elmer sounded intrigued, excited. Almost as if he were delivering the boss a plum surprise in Austin.

Austin drummed his fingers on his thigh. "How does he make money to pay you?" He forced a mirthless laugh. "Did he win the lottery?" He had been careful not to ask these questions before because they'd raise suspicions.

Elmer's lips twitched. "He didn't win the lottery." Then his expression darkened.

Austin cleared his throat. "No worries. I was raised not to discuss money." Austin hedged, carefully choosing his words. He didn't want to spook him when Austin was this close to meeting Wheeler. "I'm surprised a guy like you wouldn't want to get out and explore the world after growing up Amish."

Elmer cut him a sideways glance, hitched his shoulder, then turned his gaze back to the winding country road. He slowed as they reached the gates of the compound, seemingly stewing over something. Elmer pulled over and gave his full attention to Austin, more than he wanted.

"A guy like me?" Elmer emphasized Austin's exact choice of words, and Austin suspected he might have asked the kid one too many questions. "I can't get a good-paying job like the one I got here. Not without subjecting myself to some dumb supervisor who's clocking my breaks." He scrunched up his face in disgust. "Have you ever had the smell of cheese stuck in your nose?" He shook his head. "The work here is more meaningful." He scoffed. "Well, at least they pay me more."

Elmer put the car into drive, swung out to get a good start and gunned it up the lane, the tires spinning and the back end fishtailing. A man with a rifle—a man Austin recognized from the bar in town—dragged open the gate along a worn crescent path in the snow. Austin and Elmer continued on to the main house, the car's engine revved in low gear over the icy divots created after last night's storm.

"Keep the talk to the guns."

The guns. Why do they want them so badly? Hunting? Unlikely. Supposedly to protect themselves from desperate nonpreppers during the end days.

Austin had only gathered bits and pieces of their mission from lips loosened by one too many beers. Perhaps because it wasn't a unified plan, but more a bunch of guys and their families who leaned on each other. But now was not the time to ask.

High on the ridge, on the opposite side from the stately home that belonged to actress Jacque Caldwell, sat a white farmhouse. The house was probably built when Hunters Ridge was first settled over a hundred years ago. A huge, newer addition was designed to complement the original building.

When they climbed out, Austin went around to the back of the trunk to get the gun case, but Elmer said, "Later. Let's meet Wheeler first."

As they walked to the house, Elmer handed his car keys to Solomon Redman, the guy who seemed to be always lurking around. Now Austin had confirmation he worked for Wheeler, perhaps as the heavy. He was dressed in a camo hunting jacket. His long hair was pulled back into a ponytail. Austin watched from a distance as the man popped the trunk and took out the case with the weapon.

"Hey, wait," Austin said, trying to set the right tone, "that's mine." He pivoted and marched back toward the car. He was not going to hand over the weapon. He was using it for access, not to get someone killed. It was like walking a tightrope.

Elmer lifted an eyebrow and another man, also acting as a guard for the compound, appeared from around the side of the house aiming a gun squarely at Austin.

He dragged his gaze toward the house. Clyde Wheeler's large frame filled the doorway. Austin held up his hands, feigning concern mixed with a heaping dose of indignation. "If you're going to point that thing at me, I'm out of here."

Clyde dropped a cigarette and stubbed it out with the heel of his heavy work boot. "Lower your gun. That's no way to greet our guest."

CHAPTER 16

"Elmer, go check on the construction," Clyde said, lifting his beefy hand and pointing at a newly constructed frame with a section of heavy plastic sheeting flapping in the wind.

The spark of protest lit, then died, on Elmer's face. The kid jammed his hands into his coat pockets and hunched his shoulders as he crossed the yard covered in footprints and slushy snow and disappeared into the barn. If Elmer had thought he was valued in Clyde's eyes, he had just learned the harsh reality of it. Every interaction was transactional with Clyde.

The man in charge held up his hand, stopping Austin on the front porch, and he tilted his head toward Solomon who stood at the rear of Elmer's old clunker. Solomon approached and patted Austin down. He found Austin's gun in his ankle holster under his jeans. Without saying a word, he removed it, emptied it of bullets, and slid it into his winter coat pocket. Austin fisted his hands, reining in his emotions.

"You'll get it back later," Clyde said, stepping inside the door and disappearing.

"If you're lucky," Solomon whispered as he brushed roughly past him, setting Austin off-balance. Austin wasn't intimidated by the cocky guy's narrow build, but his weapon gave him some authority. Austin gritted his teeth. Losing his temper wasn't a good negotiating strategy. The guard stepped back and jerked his head. "Go on in."

Austin walked through the doorway, down a long hallway and into a room filled with hunting trophies. The place was more heavily protected than Austin realized. He doubted they were simply arming themselves against the townspeople who would come and steal their canned goods after they didn't prepare for the apocalypse. Something else altogether was going on here. Something more than potentially dealing in weed. He felt it in his gut.

The wood floor creaked under Austin's boots as he followed Clyde deeper into the house. About a half dozen bucks mounted on the wall were staring back at him. The stocky man plopped down on a swivel chair and leaned back. The chair groaned. He threaded his fingers and rested them on his extended belly. "The Graber kid seems to have taken a liking to you."

Austin crossed his arms over his chest and shrugged. "Nice kid."

The older man lifted his head, smoothing out the loose skin under his chin. "Graber thinks you have something we might want."

"One of your guys already has his mitts on my things. I don't like that."

Clyde laughed, a wet, popping sound that broke into a coughing fit. He pounded on his chest with his fist and smiled. "Damn habit is going to kill me."

Austin doubted a man like Clyde would live long enough to die by some horribly slow disease.

Clyde took a minute to compose himself. "I can appreciate a man who doesn't like when his possessions are handled, but you have to understand I need to know what you have."

"I can tell you exactly what I have." Austin infused icy steel into his tone. "All you have to do is ask."

"Please." The single word held the same amount of resoluteness. Clyde picked up the pack of cigarettes on the table, then set them down, perhaps thinking better of it. "Why do you have these weapons?"

Austin moved his gaze to the open doorway behind Clyde where one of his man handled Austin's weapon. "I like to do target practice." He hated to arm these men—any more than they were already armed—and he hoped a high-enough price, but not too high, would keep them interested but prevent him from having to deliver too soon, or at all. He was here for information, but had to barter in something much deadlier.

"I also like target practice." Clyde held out his palm and the man from the other room came in and handed him the weapon. He set it on the desk. Austin didn't miss the threatening tone.

"Join me some time," Austin said, throwing off a vibe that he didn't care one way or another.

"Perhaps," Clyde emphasized Austin's choice of words, "you could procure a few weapons for me and my friends, so we could all practice." He coughed again. "We need to be prepared."

"What are you preparing for?"

"We live in an unstable world." Clyde palmed the wood arms of his chair. It groaned under his weight as he leaned back. "Austin Young, retired lieutenant from the US Army, you must have experienced some of this unrest firsthand."

Ah, the man had done his research on Austin. "Just looking for a peaceful place to live." He had been correct in not asking Elmer directly about Chris. Word would have gotten back to Wheeler, dashing all hopes of ever gaining access to the compound. Never finding answers.

"Even a small town isn't always safe." The man's ominous tone scurried across his flesh like a cockroach spooked by the sudden flip of a light switch in a cold bathroom in the middle of the night.

"Yeah," Austin said noncommittally. "I suppose that's why I have weapons."

"How can I gain some of this security?" Clyde let his words trail off while his eyes studied him closely.

Before Austin had a chance to say anything more, he heard a commotion at the door. A moment later, Elmer came barging into the room. Despite being dismissed by Clyde earlier, he must have been hanging out close by. He had his cell phone in his hand and a mix of apology and rage on his face. "We have to go," he said to Austin.

"What's going on?" Clyde asked, his eyes narrowing.

"That..." Elmer pursed his lips. He looked like he wanted to spit nails. "My sister called from her job at the lumberyard. Deputy Flagler was out at my house looking for me. That woman needs to learn her place."

"What does she have against you, Elmer?" Clyde asked. It seemed the man missed nothing.

Elmer's face grew red and Austin jumped in. "She was harassing me, too. Probably being a lady cop she has something to prove. I've seen it in the military." If Elmer got booted from the compound because he was drawing too much heat, Austin might also lose his precarious "in."

Maybe. Unless Clyde wanted what he had to offer. But it was unlikely that a man with his connections wouldn't have less risky inroads to weapons.

"Looks like we're going to have to keep an eye on her," Clyde said, calmly folding his hands over his belly again.

Despite his casual gesture, something unnerving swept across his face.

The guard by the door glanced down at his phone, then looked up, clearly agitated. "There's a sheriff's patrol car down at the gate. I'll tell them to turn them away."

Clyde's eyes slid past Austin, then returned to his guard. "Do you have a name?"

The man spoke into the phone, then back to Clyde. "Deputy Flagler."

Austin's stomach dropped out. What was she doing here?

CHAPTER 17

Caitlin was forced to stop at the gate blocking the driveway to the compound. She pushed the patrol door open and climbed out. A brisk breeze caught her and made her shudder. A man stepped out from the tree line with a shotgun pointed down by his side. Her fingers twitched by her gun on her hip. *Easy.*

She hiked up her chin. "I'm looking for Clyde Wheeler."

The man stepped back and took a phone call. Apparently whoever he called hadn't protested her arrival because after a brief wait, the guard unlatched the gate and pulled it open. What was on this compound that demanded this kind of security? Was it simply part of being prepared for anything? It seemed extreme, but so did the whole concept of preparing for anarchy.

She scanned the property as she drove up the winding lane and then burst into an opening. Cars lined the driveway, mostly SUVs, trucks, and Jeeps. An impressive farmhouse squatted on the land, new construction on the far side of the house. Diffused lighting bled through the thick plastic tacked to the unfinished structure to block out the arctic cold. Drawing in a quick, fortifying breath, she climbed out of her SUV and adjusted her hat. Power tools whirred and echoed in the otherwise still country air. The door on the main house swung open and a stocky man stepped out.

Clyde Wheeler.

He angled his head, studying her. She sensed, rather than saw, another man standing inside, near him in the shadows. Pinpricks blanketed her scalp as the adrenaline coursing through her veins made her hyperaware. She cleared her throat. "Clyde Wheeler."

"The one and only," he said. "How can I help you, deputy?"

"I'm looking for an Amish youth, Elmer Graber."

Clyde's gaze drifted over to his left, in the direction of the construction. "I employ a lot of Amish men. They're handy. Hard to find the skill nowadays." He smiled, an expression that came off oily, lacking in sincerity. "I don't know all their names. They come and go."

Caitlin took a step forward. "I'll look around. His family is worried."

"Did this…" Clyde made a show of trying to remember something. "Did this Elmer person do something wrong?"

"He's been in trouble in the past."

"And now? What has he done?" Skepticism weighed heavily in his tone.

A steady current of foreboding thrummed through her veins. She couldn't flat-out lie. Well, perhaps bending the truth a bit would be allowed. "Nothing. Like I said, his family is worried. I'd like to set their minds at ease. Let them know he's okay, especially after the Aaron Miller incident."

"Is that the poor Amish kid who died in the hunting accident?" Clyde tilted his head and squinted up at the thick snow clouds. "Shame. Not sure what that has to do with me."

Caitlin studied his face. This guy was enjoying toying with her. "Miller worked here."

"Like I said, I employ a lot of Amish. Sheriff Littlefield was up here investigating. Just a tragic accident." Clyde flipped up his collar and zipped up his thick winter coat all the way. "I'd be happy to talk to the sheriff directly if you'd like."

Caitlin squared her shoulders. Being dismissed was a common occurrence. Despite it being the third decade in a new century, many people, especially in a small town, didn't take to female deputies. But she felt like there was something more to this. Something confirming the whispers in her department. Did Wheeler have Littlefield in his pocket, or was this Wheeler's passive-aggressive way of undermining Caitlin's authority?

"Since I'm here..." She held out her hand and smiled brightly, feeling her face was going to crack with the insincerity of it.

Without saying a word, Clyde stepped back into the house. Caitlin furrowed her brow. Had he just dismissed her? She turned in a slow circle, scanning the landscape. The view of Hunters Ridge from here was spectacular, even in winter. The spire of the church on Main Street was partially visible in the distance between the bare tree branches. She turned back around. Behind the main house were a few outbuildings in various states of disrepair. Footpaths in the snow crisscrossed the land. A lot of activity out here. Perhaps her first inquiry to Clyde shouldn't have been about Elmer, but rather a pointed question about what exactly was going on here. He certainly wouldn't have given her a truthful answer, but his reply might have been revealing all the same.

Inwardly, she scolded herself. She was smarter than that.

Understanding that yes, she had been dismissed—and realizing she had no recourse—she made for her SUV. The door of the house opened and a young man in a green army jacket and worn jeans stepped out onto the porch. It took her a second to recognize him. *Elmer Graber.*

The Amish kid scrubbed a hand over his head and his poorly cut hair poked out of his knit hat in disheveled tufts. When it became apparent he wasn't going to speak, Caitlin took a step toward him. "Your family is worried about you."

Something in her words seemed to spark action in the young man. He strode toward her with a sense of purpose that made her fingers flex over the butt of her gun.

She held up her hand. "Stop there, Elmer."

He drew up short, perhaps surprised by her steely command. His dark eyes grew to black pools. "My *dat*'s not worried about me." Despite the anger etched in his face, his statement smelled of desperation. "You're lying. I've done nothing wrong. Leave me alone."

"Your mother must be worried, too. She's already suffered so much loss." Caitlin's face flushed at using his dead sister as leverage.

"My family would never send a deputy to look for me." The Amish rarely got law enforcement involved in their affairs. *Be in this world, not of it.* "I come home when I need to."

"Don't do this to your family," Caitlin pressed, hoping something would get him talking.

He twisted his mouth. "Whatever."

This conversation was not proving fruitful. "Elmer," she lowered her voice, "what type of work are you doing up here? You've been on probation for harassing Violet Jackson, then your DUI. You can't risk going afoul of the law again. Prison wouldn't be kind to you."

His lips twitched and he spit out, "Construction."

"Did you know Aaron Miller?"

"Of course." He jerked his head back as if saying *pfft*. His response didn't seem to jibe with the question.

"Do you know anything about his death?" Her gaze drifted over his shoulder to the empty porch. A curtain fluttered in the window. They were being watched.

"Hunting accident." His tone had a flat affect, as if he was repeating an untruth.

"I understand Aaron didn't like to hunt."

Elmer's stoic expression faltered for a fraction before his mouth pursed. "I don't know nothing about that."

"Are you sure? You seem to know Mr. Wheeler well enough to be visiting with him in the house while construction is going on. You're not working."

He glanced nervously over his shoulder. "I had to check in about…something."

"What are you afraid of?" Caitlin pressed, sensing the man's frustration. He was usually arrogant and full of himself.

He snapped his gaze back toward her. "Why are you harassing me?"

"You're not naive. You can't claim you don't know any better. Not anymore." Her pulse thrummed in her neck and she tried to push aside her personal grievances. She had zero tolerance for drunk drivers. For the likes of Elmer Graber.

"I've already been punished for the stuff I did." He took a step backward, a smug expression on his face.

The stuff? "What about the slaughtered pig on Eve Reist's doorstep?"

"What-t-t…" Elmer stammered for the first time.

"You haven't been charged for that." She left the word *yet* unspoken. He might deny it, but the guilt was written all over his face.

He shook his head in disgust. "Arrest me if you have proof. Otherwise leave me alone."

Caitlin yanked open the door of her SUV as anger heated her cheeks. "Then I'll be back when I have proof." She climbed behind the wheel of the SUV and she and Elmer glared at one another. She looked away first and started the engine and jammed the gear into reverse. The guard had the gate open at the bottom of the lane, as if someone had called down to him that she was on her way out.

When Caitlin reached the country road, she allowed her shoulders to relax. She had allowed her dislike of Elmer's actions to color her thinking, causing her to lose her temper. She tapped her fist on her steering wheel. If Clyde had some sort of friendship with the sheriff like Wanda had mentioned, Caitlin might get reprimanded for harassing the members of his compound. The sheriff had already clearly told his deputies to leave it alone.

This wouldn't be good for her career.

Caitlin pressed the accelerator, her gaze sharply focused on the road in front of her. No, she was onto something and she wouldn't allow anyone to bully her into letting it go.

Not even her boss.

CHAPTER 18

"She is such a witch," Elmer complained, his rage rolling off him in waves. "Such a—"

"Whoa, what happened out there?" Austin held up his hand, stopping his driver mid-curse. "Was that sheriff's deputy here for you? I thought all your legal problems were behind you, man." The knot that had formed between his shoulder blades the second he had realized Deputy Caitlin Flagler had arrived at the compound had begun to ease. She was gone. She was safe.

For now.

Why did he care so much? He had only met her a few days ago.

"She's got her nose in places it doesn't belong." Elmer was enraged.

"Ah, she's just doing her job. A peon like us. Following orders for the boss." Austin tried to calm the kid's nerves. Elmer had been known to make bad decisions, and Austin didn't want any of them to be directed toward the pretty deputy.

Elmer scoffed. "Not likely." His mouth twitched as he put

the car into drive and had to rock it out of a snowy rut outside the compound.

"What do you mean?" Austin pressed.

Elmer cut him a sideways glance, then went back to cussing and grumbling until he finally got some forward momentum, his tires gaining purchase on the patches of gravel poking through the snow.

When Caitlin had first arrived on the compound, Clyde's guard had prevented Austin from going outside with Elmer. If Austin had protested, he might have shined too bright a light on himself. So he lingered inside, feeling the eyes of the guard on him while Clyde hovered at the window, watching the exchange between Elmer and the deputy. Austin acted casual while his skin buzzed with adrenaline. He'd felt like he was so close to making inroads to finding out what happened to Chris Rutherford when he was forced to take a step back. These guys spooked easily. He could sense it. He had itched to find out what was happening outside, but Clyde blocked his view, perhaps not intentionally. Unfortunately, Austin couldn't make out the context of the muted conversation.

The men hadn't made any concrete plans regarding the guns, but Austin was confident he had a foot in the door. He had to make sure the door didn't get slammed shut before he got a chance to snoop around. Ask questions. Now, Austin could only pry information from Elmer. See why the deputy had him so riled up.

Elmer slowed at the gate on their way off the property and pounded his fist on the steering wheel. The guard held up his hand. The kid cranked the window down with the jerky movements of someone clearly annoyed.

"*Yah*, what is it?" Elmer asked curtly.

Just then a different man lumbered out of a pathway between the trees with a duffel bag slung over his shoulder.

Solomon Redman. Again. He had met him more than once at the bar in town. He wasn't receptive to Austin's overtures of free drinks and friendship. No, he was hard-nosed. A loose cannon. Adrenaline surged in Austin's veins. He shifted in his seat. The majestic pine trees blocked the view of the house under construction.

"Solomon needs a ride into town," the guard said.

The man didn't wait for a reply from Elmer. He yanked on the handle and the door flung open and he hopped in, bringing in a dank smell. Austin glanced over his shoulder at their new passenger, then at Elmer who didn't protest. The guard peeled open the gate across the frozen landscape. The guard didn't look cold, despite having a position out in the elements, making Austin suspect there was a shelter nearby, perhaps an outbuilding hidden by the mature pine trees.

Elmer ignored Solomon, so Austin said, "Where you headed?"

"Into town. I have to pick up a few things at the hardware store." An odor reminiscent of aged cheese wafted off the man's clothing. Then he turned his focus to Elmer. "That woman still after you?"

That woman?

"She's got nothing on me," Elmer ground out. "Nothing."

"Then I suppose you've got nothing to worry about." Solomon's statement sounded ominous. Was that why Clyde had sent him off the ridge to catch a ride into town with them? To get dirt on Austin? Or to watch Elmer? Or to threaten the deputy directly?

"She's harassing me about that stupid pig again. If she thinks that was a threat…" Elmer let the warning drift off, but Austin didn't think he was doing it for his benefit. It was more like he was lost deep in his thoughts.

"We can put an end to it," Solomon said. Austin turned his

head. The man was fingering a gun in his unzipped duffel bag.

"She's a sheriff's deputy. You can't touch her," Austin said, trying to act casual. "Messing with law enforcement will bring too much heat."

Solomon lifted his dark gaze. "Are you talking from experience?"

"Nope. I keep my nose clean."

"Unless you're selling guns." Something in Solomon's tone sounded unhinged. He shifted to look at Elmer. "Wouldn't be hard to fix this problem."

Austin felt a muscle twitching in his jaw, but he had to maintain his cool.

So close to making his way into the compound. Finding out what happened to Chris.

Solomon slid forward and tapped the back of the seat. "Just drop me in town. Pick me up in an hour." Before Solomon climbed out in front of the hardware store, he said, "Clyde doesn't like complications. Or loose ends. I hear she lives alone."

Austin watched the man climb out and then turn around and lock gazes with him. A flicker of a smile tugged at the corners of his mouth, then disappeared. *Punk.*

Elmer pulled away from the curb, his agitation still oppressive in the small space. "She's had it out for me ever since I got stopped. Told me I was drunk. It was all a setup. Then she accused me of putting a slaughtered pig on the Reist farm." The tough leather of the steering wheel let out a woof under his fist. "Solomon might be right."

Austin decided to play it another way. He chuckled, forcing amusement into his tone, as if he thought Elmer's actions were humorous. "Well, she doesn't have to go far to put the pieces together. Your family does own a pig farm?"

Elmer laughed, an ugly sound. "It was easy money. And no one got hurt."

"Has Clyde asked you to do anything for him?"

Elmer scrubbed a hand over his face, seemingly hesitant.

"You know you can trust me. I bailed you out of jail, remember?"

"Is that why you did it, so you could ask me for favors?"

Austin sighed. "Listen, I'm new in town. I don't know many people. And once I make friends, I look out for them. I haven't asked you for anything."

"Clyde's careful with who he associates with. I'm this close—" he lifted his fingers an inch apart "—to being one of his trusted men."

"Trusted to do what?"

Elmer pulled up in front of the place Austin was renting. "Here you go." He climbed out and popped the trunk. "Don't forget what you came with." He pivoted and strode away from him without saying another word.

"Elmer?"

The kid tapped his fist on the roof of the car. "I'm not going to let her ruin everything I've worked for."

CHAPTER 19

The branches over Austin's head clacked in the wicked breeze, and he shuddered. He adjusted the collar of his thick coat and lifted the binoculars to survey Deputy Caitlin Flagler's house. Freshly fallen snow whirled over the frozen land surrounding her property.

Austin didn't know Solomon well enough to know if he'd go through with his threat to harass the deputy, but he had a gut feeling this guy was unhinged. He sank deeper into his coat and tried to relax his shoulders.

Don't think about the cold.

Caitlin was a complication he hadn't counted on. He came here to track down Chris, but now he felt compelled to protect a woman he barely knew. He let out a long breath. He might not have known her, but he was familiar with the knucklehead types who were egging each other on to put a deputy in her place. Elmer and his buddy, Solomon, were the kind of guys who, once they had an ax to grind, wouldn't let it go. They were determined to sharpen it on Caitlin. Might gain them credentials with their peers, or even Clyde Wheeler.

He couldn't take the chance of something happening to her when he had prior knowledge. Yet he couldn't come right out and tell her because he had invested too much time in this investigation that hadn't yet gotten results. He'd watch over her. Keep his mouth shut. Unless his hand was forced.

Precipitation landed on the lens of the binoculars, enhancing the snow globe effect of the landscape. He scanned the surrounding area again. She had one neighbor to the right, about a hundred feet from her house. No other visible neighbors. From as far as he could tell, the neighbor was an elderly gentleman who seemed content to sit in front of the TV for the past ninety minutes, the length of Austin's watch.

A stiff breeze caught the small, uncovered patch of skin under his beard. A new shudder raced up his spine. He had withstood far worse extremes than this in Afghanistan, but man, he was getting too old for this. He let his gaze shift back to the neighbor's house. He lowered the binoculars, then lifted them again. The gentleman wasn't in his chair. He directed the focus of his binoculars to the driveway and a second later a side light popped on. He squinted. Red hair. Nice figure. *Caitlin.* "Hmmm?"

He watched the neighbors chat. The old man handed her something. They talked a little more. She waved goodbye, put whatever he had given her into her SUV, then she hoisted the garbage tote into the back of his pickup truck before driving it to the curb. She returned to switch vehicles and left. Apparently she was one of those do-gooders, helping out her elderly neighbor. He smiled to himself. Something he refused to acknowledge swirled in his gut. He trained the binoculars on her taillights as she drove away. He lost sight of her for a second, then her headlights reappeared in her driveway.

Austin drew his arms in close to his body and shuddered

to generate some body heat. She disappeared behind her garage, then appeared with her blue garbage tote. He could descend from the woods now and warn her, but what if someone was watching the house? He couldn't take that chance and blow his cover. It would be less risky if he just watched. Made sure those clowns didn't try anything.

She returned from the base of the driveway, grabbed something out of her truck, then let herself in by the side door. Once she made it inside, he had a clear view through the large windows. Apparently she didn't feel the need for blinds, what with no neighbors living behind her. Definitely a mistake. He lowered the binoculars, feeling a bit voyeuristic. Even without them, he caught glimpses of her moving around what he suspected was the kitchen. He couldn't help but wonder why a woman like her lived alone. Then he checked himself. He had met plenty of strong, independent women. None of them needed a man to make their life complete.

Austin crossed his arms over his chest and waited. An uneasiness ticked in his head. He couldn't protect her forever. Maybe there was some way to warn her without being detected by prying eyes.

But would she trust him enough to keep his secret?

CHAPTER 20

Caitlin's house smelled like Mr. C's chili. She had warmed a small bowl in the microwave but didn't want to eat too much before crawling into bed. She had stopped over to visit Olivia after work, and the two of them ended up chatting for a few hours. They both needed the friendship to unwind from their days, even now, as they were so different.

Caitlin smiled to herself as she snuggled between the soft sheets, thanks to her electric blanket. This was absolutely her favorite time of day. Her warm bed, her comfy PJ's and a book. Every week for as long as she could remember, her elderly neighbor made her dinner for the simple favor of taking his garbage tote down to the end of the long driveway. She would have done it for free, but she wasn't one to turn down food. And she understood that Mr. C didn't want her charity.

She got that more than most.

With her mind still racing from the recent events of her job, she picked up her latest romance novel sitting on the end table. Her coworkers would probably harass her if they knew her favorite genre was sweet romance, but she really didn't care. She needed the escape and the promise of happily ever after. Because goodness knew, she hadn't had a lot of that in her life.

After a few pages, the words began to swirl, so she slid a bookmark to hold her spot and set the book down. She reached over and shut off the light. Her bedroom was cast in darkness, but unlike the loud summer critters, the room was filled with the eerie silence of winter, intermittently broken up by a swift wind and the creaking of her little house in the woods. The stillness always sent her back to her childhood. Lying in bed, maybe at age ten or eleven—far too young to be left alone at night—waiting for her mother to arrive home from the bar. Every noise was an intruder lurking outside her bedroom ready to hack her to pieces. She really should have laid off the horror movies at Halloween, and perhaps the steady diet of true crime shows hadn't been a good idea for a young girl. But her fascination—and a myriad of other influences—shaped her into the woman she was today.

Caitlin rolled over and pulled her comforter up over her bare shoulder and laughed to herself. Her childhood experiences stayed with her, making her feel uneasy in the dark of night. As a child, she thought a comforter over her head would protect her from the boogeyman. Now, she had her personal gun stashed away in her bedside table.

Real protection.

With that knowledge, her body relaxed, and her mother's pretty face floated to mind, as it often did when Caitlin was in that hazy zone between awake and asleep. Her mother was most upbeat when she had on "her face," as she called it, ready for a night out. Caitlin thought her mother was more beautiful without the heavy makeup, dressed casually, and working in the garden. But that version of her mother was never around for long before her party mom returned. Caitlin hated to be left alone, but more than that she hated when her mother brought her men home. She rolled over and tried to shake the memory.

Caitlin wished her mother could see her cozy house, similar to what her mother used to dream for the two of them, even as she struggled to pay the rent on a small duplex in town. Her mother, who had only begun what was sure to be a long climb out of her own bad choices when a celebratory night backsliding into too much to drink had ended her life. And forever changed Caitlin's.

She wasn't sure how long she had been drifting off when she heard a creak. Not the same as the usual settling sounds of her house. And she had memorized every sound. Her heart raced in her ears, even as her mind objectively considered her next move. Her eyes searched the black.

Silently, she peeled back the covers and scanned the darkness. Despite the shadows, she couldn't see anything out of place. But she felt something. Something was off. She slid open the drawer. The cold metal of the gun put steel in her spine.

"Who's there?" She shouted the command in the most authoritative voice she could muster. Her hand twitched on the gun, her finger near but not on the trigger. She resisted the impulse to turn on the light. She was familiar with her own home. That was her advantage over a potential intruder. Her bare feet were silent on the drafty hardwood floor as she moved swiftly toward the bedroom door.

Someone was definitely there.

"I'm a sheriff's deputy. Show yourself." Her voice cracked. "Now!"

"I'm not going to hurt you." A disembodied voice floated to her from somewhere in the direction of her kitchen. She lifted the gun and pointed down the dark hallway.

"Stay where you are," she commanded, a shiver racing up her spine despite her best efforts to be tough.

"I won't, Deputy Flagler. I—"

"Who are you?" He knew her name. She froze for a half beat, trying to think as adrenaline flooded her veins. All she could hear was her own heavy breathing. He could be anyone. Lots of locals knew her name. "Why are you in my house?" She was not going to be a victim in her own home. The bizarre thought that she'd never be able to live that down bounced around her head. If she was dead, it wouldn't matter.

"You're in danger," he said. Something familiar about his voice whispered across her brain. "You have to trust me."

"I don't even know you."

"I'm not going to turn on a light because I believe someone may be watching the house."

Caitlin's stomach dropped and her weapon hand trembled. She had never fired it at another human being. She hiked her chin. *Fake it till you make it.* "Talk fast," she bit out.

"It's Austin. Austin Young."

The man who had crossed her path a few times in the past few days. The man she had dinner with at Olivia's.

"Why did you break into my house?" Now she wished she had grabbed her phone from her nightstand so she could call dispatch. Wanda.

"You were at the compound today," Austin said.

The fine hairs on the back of her neck prickled to life with that simple statement. "How do you know that?"

"I was there."

Her stomach dropped. "So you're tied to that operation?"

"That's not important." His tone grew more urgent. "Someone from the compound wants to hurt you. We need to go now."

Caitlin was getting really mad. "I'm not going with you.

Anywhere." Her self-defense training had told her victims of crime were more likely to be killed if they left with their attacker. She supposed it didn't matter if he claimed to be trying to save her life.

What kind of messed-up game is he playing?

The moonlight sliced across his face as he risked a step closer to her. A muscle ticked in his jaw. "We're running out of time."

Something in his desperate look made a fresh surge of adrenaline jack up her heart rate. Just then, glass exploded somewhere in the house. Austin lunged toward her and wrapped his arm around her waist and made her move with him away from the sound. With his back pressed against the wall, he peered into the kitchen. By the way he was holding her, she too got a glimpse of the scene. Someone had thrown a brick through the window on the side door. They were now slamming something against it, trying to force their way in.

"You've got to come with me now!" he said in a hushed voice. "There's no time."

Stimulation overload made it hard to think clearly. "No," she growled. "I'm a deputy. I'm not going to let someone break into my home."

"I can't let you expose me."

"What?"

Frustration and something she couldn't quite read flashed across his face. "Come with me now. I'll explain everything to you." She wasn't budging. "You trust Drew, right? We're friends. You know that. Trust me." His urgent plea was accompanied by a relentless slamming, echoing through her house. Whoever wanted in wasn't worried about being sly about it. Maybe they were drunk or on drugs. A looming shadow of her mother's mean-drunk boyfriends made icy dread pool in her gut.

Caitlin swallowed hard and nodded, in that moment making a split-second decision.

"Is there another way out of here?" Austin asked.

"Through the basement. There's an exit at the back of the house."

"Do you have boots and a coat nearby?"

"Mudroom off the kitchen next to the fridge." Her lower lip quivered. An ax murderer wouldn't want her to grab her coat and boots, right? Thank goodness the deadbolt and steel door was holding. Only the small panes of glass near the top had given way.

Caitlin grabbed her boots and coat and hurriedly opened the cellar door off the kitchen, and Austin closed it behind them. In the basement, she turned to face him. The moonlight through the cloudy basement windows reflected in his eyes. She had to trust him.

She engaged the safety and slid the gun into her coat pocket, and jammed her arms into her sleeves, the waterproof nylon cool on her bare skin. She stuffed her feet into her boots. "Over here. The door dumps into a small outbuilding at the back of the property. The previous owners did a lot of canning and used the extra space for storage in the winter," she whispered. The sound of heavy footsteps overhead made her blood run cold. *They made it in!*

When she and Austin reached the door to the outside, Caitlin shuddered. A cold, snowy field extended between them and the tree line.

"We've got to make a run for it," Austin said.

Through the cracks in the floorboards of the old cabin, Caitlin heard someone cursing her out. She turned and looked up at the man she had only met a few days ago but who seemed to be a central part of her life, and said, "Let's go." She ducked her head and ran toward the trees. Austin followed close behind. When they reached cover, Caitlin planted her bare hand on the bark and drew in a deep breath. The air was so cold it hurt her lungs. A draft found its way under her coat. "Now what?" Again, she was annoyed with herself for not grabbing her cell phone.

"This way. My truck is a few hundred feet in on the small service road."

"Thank you, God," Caitlin whispered and lifted her frozen, wet foot to take another step.

CHAPTER 21

The four-wheel drive plowed through the snow on the infrequently traveled road that wound through the woods behind Caitlin's house. Over the few years that she had lived here, she saw more hikers than drivers on this path. She reached into her coat pocket and touched her handgun.

"You don't need that," Austin said, not taking his eyes off the road, his windshield wipers swooshing against the rapidly falling snow. "At least not on account of me."

"You'll have to prove that to me." Her words trembled despite her best efforts to portray strength. She was so darn cold, even with the heat cranking out of the truck's vents. Her PJ tank top provided little warmth under her thick coat. With the initial shock of someone trying to break into her home wearing off, she was beginning to second-guess her rash decision to run off with a guy she hardly knew. How had he so easily convinced her not to call the station?

Well, there hadn't been time to grab her phone, anyway.

"Who was that breaking into my house?"

"Solomon Redman. You know him?"

"He was up at the compound today."

"Yeah." Austin cut her a quick glance, then went back to focusing on the road.

"Was he alone?" She hugged her arms tight to herself over the seat belt. What she wouldn't do to take a long, hot bath and not ask him a million questions about how he knew she had been at the compound and how he had turned up at her home at just the right time. How did he even know where she lived? *Focus.*

"Elmer Graber was with him."

Anger boiled in her gut. "That kid is always up to no good. Do they want to get back at me for drawing attention to him at the compound?" She paused a moment, pulling her thoughts together. "And how is it you're here to save me?" She should have been grateful, but her suspicion welled up and made her brush her fingers across the cool metal of her weapon.

"I'll explain everything to you. Please, just trust me." He bumped out of the narrow country lane onto the main road.

"Where are you taking me?" The trees rushed by in a blur of tangled branches against the dark sky. She held out her hand. "Give me your phone. Let me call the station."

"That's not a good idea," Austin said. The chill in his voice made her tremble.

"You want me to trust you, right? I will not go anywhere with you unless someone I truly trust knows where I am." She sat up ramrod straight in the passenger seat and reached into her pocket to touch the gun.

"How well do you know your boss?" he asked.

"The sheriff?"

"Do you trust him with your life?" He stared straight ahead at the cats' eyes marking the curve in the road.

"Say what you have to say." The intensity on his face made her look over her shoulder, but the road behind them was deserted. If Solomon and Elmer realized she had made her getaway, they had not followed in pursuit.

"I can't prove it yet, but I'm convinced Sheriff Littlefield is connected to the compound."

An awareness tickled the base of her neck. "Prepping isn't against the law, as far as I can tell." Even as she spoke the words, she realized she was repeating the sheriff's position on the compound word for word. Why was her first inclination to defend the sheriff? *Isn't that what deputies do? Fall in line?* Yet hadn't she had similar concerns? Wanda had said Wheeler had been around to see him.

Caitlin caught a mocking expression in Austin's glance. "What brought you to the compound today, then?"

"I was checking on Elmer."

"Yeah, but you're worried there's something else going on, right?"

"Yes." She studied his heavily shadowed profile. "Who are you, really?"

He focused his attention on the road. "FBI."

"What?" Her heart rate spiked. Her own sheriff had denied the preppers were doing anything illegal, yet now the feds were involved? She was surprised by the anger welling up inside her. "Why didn't you show me your FBI credentials when I was called to your house the other night?"

"I'll explain everything at the cabin."

"Cabin? The farmhouse you're renting?"

"I'm not taking you there. I have a place deep in the woods. It's off the grid." He sounded matter-of-fact, not like some deranged serial killer. "My bugout shelter."

"You sound like one of them."

He hitched his shoulder noncommittally. Probably part of his cover story.

"I'm not going to some isolated cabin with you until I see some official ID." She raised her chin and steeled her voice, despite the cold seeping into her bones. She couldn't let whatever this little attraction between them was cloud her judgment. She had gotten out of more than one sticky situation as a female deputy in a small town where the occasional rough-and-tumble guys refused direction from anyone, never mind a woman.

"Too dangerous to carry my FBI ID while undercover."

"This doesn't feel right to me."

"I saved you back there. I'd think that would buy me some credit." Austin slowed and glanced in the rearview mirror. Apparently satisfied that no one was following, he turned off the country road. He shifted the gear on his 4x4 and floored it. His snow tires chewed up the path that hadn't yet been plowed. Probably wouldn't be cleared all winter. "If I wanted to see you hurt, I could have left you in the hands of Elmer and Solomon."

Caitlin's blood ran cold at the memory of the banging at the side door. "I have a gun. I could have handled myself."

"I didn't want to wait and see." He tipped his head. "Sorry."

Ignoring his comment, she asked, "How do you know these guys coming after me has to do with Wheeler and not just their own beef with me?"

Austin navigated the vehicle into a structure that had seen better days, perhaps to keep it out of sight. "I heard the men talking about you on the way down the ridge. Yeah, they're mad at you, for sure, but I'm convinced Clyde uses what he knows about people to have them do his bidding. I figured they weren't the patient type, so I hunkered down in the woods behind your house. As soon as I saw a car drive past your place, slow down and turn around, I slipped in."

Caitlin rubbed her forehead and glanced over at him. "How did you get in so easily while they tried to get in like they were using a bulldozer?"

"Your house isn't as secure as you might think."

She tried not to take his slam personally, since he had gotten in undetected. "Maybe if your job with the FBI doesn't work out, you can go into home security."

A deep chuckle rumbled up from his throat. Despite herself, she liked the sound of it. "I don't think so."

"I still think we should call the sheriff. He might not want to rile up the Amish or interfere with the compound, but he'd never tolerate one of his own getting harassed." *Would he?*

"I need you to hear me out. Then you can decide." Austin adjusted the heat and asked, "Warm enough?"

Caitlin held up her hand to the vent. "Not yet."

"I can build a fire in the cabin."

Suddenly the idea of sitting by a roaring fire with this man sounded more appealing than it probably should. She rested her elbow on the door frame and rolled her eyes in the dark. She shoved aside any romantic notions and forced as much steel as she could into her voice. "And then you're going to tell me everything."

CHAPTER 22

*A*ustin threw another log on the fire, and tiny embers rained down. He'd have to take his chances that someone might notice the smoke coming out of the chimney. That was far less risky than freezing to death in this drafty cabin. He glanced over his shoulder at Caitlin, who was sitting cross-legged on the couch with the hood on her winter coat up, the dark faux fur framing her mussed red hair and pretty face. She had been very quiet since they arrived. Perhaps she was plotting her next move. Or wondering about his. He didn't take her for someone who waited for things to happen. And he couldn't risk her actions unraveling six weeks of undercover work.

He hooked the fire poker on the stand and turned to face her. He imagined prior to learning he was FBI she had taken him for one of those paranoid loner types steeped in conspiracy theories. Sure, it wasn't hard to believe two lowlifes had it out for someone in law enforcement, but he had to convince her that something bigger was going on at the compound. Something that might motivate someone to remove all obstacles.

"You warm enough?" he asked.

Caitlin hadn't moved. Her chin was tucked into the collar of her winter coat. She tipped her head at him and opened her eyes wide, as if to say, *What do you think?* She had her arms crossed tightly in front of her, giving off a completely unapproachable vibe.

"I'm sorry you got wrapped up in this." Austin disappeared into the other room and returned with a thick quilt. He tossed it on the couch next to her. He lowered himself onto the edge of the coffee table, careful to give her space.

She cut him a sideways, suspicious look. She toed off her boots and set them off to the side. She wrapped the quilt around her, folding her feet under her. "I hate being cold."

"I'm not a fan of it either." The heat from the fireplace warmed his back. He turned and peered out the window, the only reflection its orange glow. "I think it's snowing hard enough to cover our tracks. No one will follow us up here."

"Would either of them suspect you're helping me?" Her question was filled with cynicism, as if she didn't believe he was actually helping her.

"I hope not, because if I blow this, I might never find the truth."

Caitlin unzipped her heavy winter coat, then pulled her arms out of it. She was dressed in a tank top that she had been wearing when he broke into her house. She pulled the coat out from behind her and slung it over the arm of the couch. She gathered the quilt back around her, her gaze hooded, tired.

"What truth are you looking for?" she asked around a yawn.

"I'm looking for a kid that went missing after working on the compound."

Caitlin straightened her shoulders and furrowed her brow. "You know an Amish kid died under suspicious circumstances after working for Wheeler?" She dragged a hand through her hair. "Of course you do," she said, answering her own question. "You were at the town meeting."

"I've been in town for six weeks trying to gain access to the compound. Clyde Wheeler isn't a very trustful man. He seems to let young Amish men in pretty readily to work construction, but I haven't been as fortunate."

"But you said you were up there today." She tilted her head to study him, perhaps trying to determine if he was lying.

"I was. Elmer finally made an introduction." Austin carefully chose his words.

"Why?" She untucked her legs and planted her bare toes on the hardwood floor. "Why would Elmer introduce you? To vouch for your handyman skills?" More than a trace of doubt tinged her tone.

"They're interested in some guns I have." Austin glanced out the window again. Still nothing but snow and the reflection of the fire.

"Guns? Are you serious?" She plowed a hand through her tangled hair. "The FBI authorized this?"

Austin held back some key information, afraid he'd lose her if she found out he was pursuing this case on his own. "I'm using the guns as bait. I won't give them access." Not if he could help it.

"That's a pretty dangerous game." She pulled the quilt tighter around her. "Are you on your own? Are there other undercover agents?"

"I don't want to give you too much information that you can't deny." He studied her closely.

"Now you're worried about my career?" She shook her head in disbelief. "Kidnap me in the middle of the night, tell me the FBI is running an operation without local law enforcement's knowledge, and tell me I can't tell anyone. You're putting me in an awful position." She jerked her chin toward him. "Why don't you show me that ID right now."

Austin pried a floorboard free and grabbed a small metal lockbox. He unlocked it and pulled out his official FBI ID and handed it to Caitlin. She turned it over in her hand. "Austin Grayson." She looked up and met his gaze. "Why didn't you tell me you were FBI when I came out to your place the night of the disturbance call? I could have shot your head off."

"But you didn't." He hiked an eyebrow and watched her closely, growing somber. "I didn't know who I could trust."

"And now you know you can trust me?"

"Well, you did come up to the compound today ready to kick butt."

"True." She rewarded him with a smile. "I knew in my gut that Wheeler was up to no good." Several emotions flashed across her face. "And it's rubbed me wrong from day one that the sheriff has dismissed the locals' concerns about the compound." She assessed him carefully. "Has everything I've learned about you been a lie?"

Something in her tone felt like a sucker punch to his gut. "Not everything. I like to keep my cover story close to the truth. Harder to make mistakes."

"Like when you told Drew you were staying at your uncle's, and then later admitted you were renting from Karen Sanders?" She eyed him closely.

"That was a little flub." Austin realized Caitlin was sharp. "I *am* retired from the army. Lots of these guys on the compound are former military. It's like they're going from one brotherhood to another." He sat down on the other side of the couch, careful to give her space. "Listen, we"—technically *I*, but now was not the time to come completely clean—"believe that Clyde Wheeler is trafficking in drugs and might be paying the sheriff off to make sure he doesn't run afoul of the law. I don't know if other deputies are involved."

"Unbelievable." Caitlin leaned forward and let the quilt fall from her bare shoulders. "The sheriff has dissuaded us from 'harassing' the preppers." She turned to look him in the eyes. "What kind of drugs?"

"Marijuana, definitely." Chris had told his sister that was what they were doing, but Austin had a hard time believing that was the only drug. "Hunters Ridge provides them with proximity to the Canadian border. Acting as a preppers group is a nice distraction from the real reason they exist."

Caitlin tilted her head and scratched her cheek. "Who alerted the FBI?"

"Christopher Rutherford. Chris. I have a personal connection to the kid. He was a neighbor of mine when I was growing up. He had been hired to work there and got wind of the drugs. He casually mentioned it to his sister. He wasn't ready to give up the money, but when he disappeared, she went to Sheriff Littlefield."

Caitlin watched him expectantly.

"The sheriff said he'd look into it."

"Did he?" Caitlin had leaned forward on the couch. He could smell her shampoo.

"He claimed he did. Janelle, Chris's sister, reached out to me after she grew frustrated." He scrubbed a hand across his beard. "I had been back home clearing out my parents' place."

"You're looking for Chris?" she asked, clarifying his reasons.

"Yes."

"How do you know he didn't move on?"

Austin shook his head. "I don't think he did. He was close to his family. He simply stopped texting them. His cell phone was untraceable, too. Like someone turned it off."

"Do you have any concrete evidence the sheriff is

involved? The family's frustration in not being able to get him to act doesn't necessarily mean anything." Caitlin pushed to her feet and moved toward the window. She crossed her arms over her tank top and leaned her shoulder against the ledge and stared outside. He'd have to dig up some warmer clothes for her.

"Elmer has made hints that they can do what they want at the compound because the sheriff doesn't care."

She turned and held out her hand. "Give me your cell phone. I have to let Wanda know where I am."

Austin felt a smile pulling at his lips, but feared she might get irked if she thought she was amusing him. "It's the middle of the night. Can't it wait until morning?" The fewer people who knew, the better.

"Wanda works nights." When he didn't budge she added, "My house has been broken into. I need someone to make sure it's secure." She reached over and grabbed the quilt from where she had discarded it on the couch. She wrapped it around her bare shoulders.

"We can't alert the sheriff. He has a personal relationship with Wanda."

"You really have done your research," Caitlin said, then added, "Well, a sure way to alert the sheriff is if someone reports a break-in at my house, and I turn up missing. There will be an all-out manhunt for me."

"True enough," Austin said. "Is there someone you trust that can keep a secret?"

"Olivia and Drew, but I hate to bother them so late since they have the baby and all."

Austin ran a hand over his jaw. "I'll go. Slip in and out through the back road again. Solomon and Elmer must be long gone by now."

Caitlin didn't refuse his offer, probably because she recognized that he had put her in this situation. Maybe eventually she'd appreciate that he had saved her. He felt a smile bubbling up inside. Or maybe he would come to realize she could have handled herself.

He hadn't been ready to take that chance.

"Can you grab a few things while you're there?"

"Yes. Make it a short list. I need to get in and out. I don't want to blow my cover now."

Caitlin rattled off a few items, including her cell phone. She felt lost without it. She adjusted the pillows on the couch and leaned over and patted her coat pocket. Her gun.

Austin pushed to his feet and scrubbed a hand over his beard. "You can take the bed. I'll take the couch when I get back."

"You don't have to be all chivalrous around me." She closed her eyes and pulled the quilt up to her chin. "Just put another log on the fire before you go. And lock the door."

Austin did as she instructed. He pulled the screen across the roaring fire and then went around the cabin to make sure all the windows and doors were secure. He stood staring over the snowy landscape. He hadn't planned on bugging out to the second location he had secured in Hunters Ridge. Not this soon. But his thorough planning had come in handy. No one knew he had this place.

He'd never forgive himself if he had put someone else in jeopardy. Especially the pretty redhead sleeping on his couch.

CHAPTER 23

Caitlin had one of those nights of sleep where nonspecific dreams kept her tossing and turning. It wasn't until she had a crick in her neck and a spring poking into her thigh that she emerged fully out of her fitful sleep. The events of last night washed over her, leaving a sinking feeling in her gut.

What had Elmer and Solomon been thinking, trying to break into her house?

And was Sheriff Littlefield really protecting some sort of illegal activity on the compound?

Caitlin pushed to a seated position and rolled her shoulders. Her back might not forgive her for not taking Austin's offer of his bedroom. The smell of an old fire lingered in the air. Only a few embers still glowed. She squinted at the bird clock on the wall. If she believed the sweeping second hand indicated the clock was accurate, it was five in the morning. She moved toward the window. A vast landscape of pure white flowed into a hillside of snowy evergreens.

Caitlin cupped her bare elbows with her hands and shuddered. She glanced around and discovered a paper bag on the coffee table. She peeked in and found her hoodie and quickly shoved her arms into it and relished its warmth. Quietly, she checked the other contents: jeans, socks, and even though she hadn't explicitly asked him, he had packed undergarments. Her face flushed at the thought of him selecting her personal things from her bedroom chest of drawers. She was grateful, despite her embarrassment. She reached the bottom of the bag and couldn't find her cell phone. She muttered under her breath and more thoroughly went through all the items again.

No phone! Darn it!

She glanced over her shoulder at Austin's door. He had left it ajar. She crept in that direction. She paused at the door and listened. His steady, even breathing indicated he was asleep. If he was like most people, he probably kept his phone on the table next to his bed. Holding her breath, she pushed open the door and nearly gasped when it let out a quiet groan. She froze in place until she was assured Austin was still asleep. A sliver of moonlight between the blind and the window cut across his face.

Yeah, beards—no, *his* beard—was definitely growing on her.

She counted to ten in her head, then crept toward him, hoping her theory was right. She patted the side table and was rewarded with the cool feel of his cell phone. She touched the screen, and it scanned her face and denied her access. Undeterred, she held the phone out to his face, praying the phone would recognize him, even in this dim light.

She pulled back the phone and smiled. *Success.* She tapped her finger on the screen to keep it unlocked, then rushed out of the room. She went into the small bathroom off the kitchen and pulled the door closed, and she dialed Wanda's cell phone number.

Her friend sounded slightly hesitant. Caitlin should be grateful she answered the unfamiliar number. "Hey Wanda, it's me," she whispered. She lowered the toilet lid and sat down on the fuzzy seat cover. She didn't want to think about how many germs were on it, but she needed to sit.

"Caitlin!" Then without waiting for an answer, Wanda exclaimed, "Thank goodness. Where are you? Are you okay?"

Wanda's barrage of questions pinged around Caitlin's brain. "Yes, yes, I'm fine." If you considered being abducted out of bed in the middle of the night and brought to a cabin in the desolate woods by a handsome stranger with questionable motives as being okay, she was okay.

"Where are you?"

Caitlin pressed the phone tight to her ear. The cold tile on her feet had permeated her entire body. She stood, crept out of the bathroom, and peered out the kitchen window. Her exhalation fogged the glass. "I'm fine." Unease gathered at the back of her neck. "Why do you sound so concerned?"

"Your neighbor called in about a break-in at your house last night. And you weren't answering your cell phone."

"Oh man, I didn't mean to make you worry. I made it out okay, but I don't have my phone." Sweet Mr. C had been looking out for her. "Can someone run by and let him know everything's all right?" She rubbed the back of her neck. "Did they do a lot of damage to my house?"

"Dylan went out. They broke the window on the side door. Jim said he'd board it up." *The sheriff.*

Caitlin swallowed her displeasure. "How did they get in?"

"Through one of the windows. Jim will take care of that, too." Wanda let out a rush of breath. "Why didn't you come right to the station? Where are you?"

"I can't tell you." And that was the truth. "But I'm safe." She hoped.

"What's going on? Who are you with?"

"No more questions, Wanda. I just wanted you to know I'm safe. I shouldn't tell you anything else." Caitlin tossed a glance over her shoulder. No sign of Austin. She kept her voice low. She had to give her dear friend something. "You have to keep this secret."

"Tell me right now!" Wanda said sharply.

Caitlin trusted Wanda more than anyone. She took a deep breath before saying, "There's speculation the compound is trafficking in drugs and..." The next words got stuck in her throat. "Please, just take this for what it is, but the sheriff may be looking the other way." Silence stretched across the line for a heartbeat. "Wanda?" Caitlin knew her friend and Jim had a personal relationship, but Wanda was also pragmatic.

"No, that can't be," Wanda whispered.

Heat flushed Caitlin's cheeks. She hated to disappoint Wanda. Caitlin cleared her throat. "They're still investigating. Maybe..." She swallowed the strong need to defend the sheriff, if only to placate her dear friend.

"Who is we?" Wanda asked, her tone of disbelief turned inquisitive. "What are you up to, Caitlin?"

"I shouldn't have said anything." She glanced over her shoulder across the open floor plan of the cabin to Austin's bedroom door, then immediately back toward the window. She dragged her finger along the condensation warping the old wood frame. "Please keep this to yourself. Just tell the sheriff I'm okay. That I took a few vacation days and I'll be visiting friends in Buffalo and—" A warm hand on her arm made her stop midsentence. Austin stood next to her barechested, his hair mussed from sleep. She had been so engrossed by the conversation that she hadn't heard his approach.

A hot flush of awareness raced over her skin. Caitlin wasn't sure if it was because she had been caught making a phone call, or because her host was standing in front of her in a state of undress that did things to her insides.

Austin shook his head slightly. "Don't say any more," he whispered, so only she could hear him.

"Caitlin?" Wanda said. "Tell me what's going on."

"Um…" In that moment, she decided to fully trust Austin, an FBI agent, over her own boss, a man she had long held reservations about. She looked up and met Austin's unwavering gaze.

"Wanda, I'm fine. Please don't worry about me. And please keep this quiet."

"Be careful, Caitlin." An alert sounded in the background. Dispatch. "I have an incoming call. I have to go."

"Bye, Wanda." Caitlin held out the phone to Austin. "Here."

Austin took his phone, and their fingers brushed in the exchange. Caitlin ignored the surge of electricity that raced up her arm. Self-consciously, she played with the zipper on her hoodie, grateful she had thrown it on over her PJ tank.

"Wanda Reynolds has a romantic relationship with Sheriff Littlefield." He really had been digging into things here in Hunters Ridge.

"I trust her completely." Wanda would choose her over her boyfriend. Wouldn't she? Caitlin felt a strange surge of jealousy born out of the broken child deep inside her.

Austin opened a kitchen drawer and pulled out her phone. "I didn't leave it with your things because I didn't want you to make any calls. Not yet, anyway."

Caitlin felt her face flush. "I couldn't let Wanda worry."

"If we're going to work together, we're going to have to trust one another. I need you to keep a low profile until I can get some answers, but you're not my prisoner." He tapped his knuckles on the countertop. "I don't want you to feel you have to sneak around. But I also request you don't make any more calls, unless it's an absolute emergency."

"Okay." Caitlin scratched her head, seemingly distracted. "Wanda said Mr. C called the sheriff's department. Did you see anyone when you went back to my house to get my things?"

Austin shook his head. "The house was empty. Maybe they had done what they needed to do and had plans to come back in the daylight. For all they knew, it was a simple break-in."

"I wonder." Caitlin's voice had a faraway quality.

"We'll figure this out." Austin pushed her cell phone toward her and shot her a look that struck her to her very core. "I'm going to shower, then I'll make breakfast."

Caitlin watched his retreating back. She wasn't sure what unnerved her more: his trust in her, or the muscles rippling across his broad shoulders as he reached into a hall closet and grabbed a clean towel. She quickly lowered her gaze before he caught her checking him out. Her attention drifted toward the window. A swirl of drifting snow danced across the frozen landscape. How long did he expect her to lie low?

She had a life. A job. And she had vowed she'd never allow a man to tell her what to do.

But something in Austin's sincere plea gave her pause.

Was this how it started?

CHAPTER 24

Austin showered, put on clean clothes, and found Caitlin sitting cross-legged on the couch with the quilt wrapped around her. She had made a fire in the fireplace and had contented herself with an old book from the shelves lining the cabin walls. He hadn't made time to explore the titles left by the previous owner.

When he entered the room, she untucked her legs and scooted to the edge of the cushion. "I appreciate your grabbing my stuff, but I still need a few more things."

He frowned. She had a point.

"I don't want to risk going back to your house. Not again. We'll drive to Buffalo or Erie and go to a superstore."

He went to the kitchen area and pulled a cast iron pan off a hook. "I hope you like bacon." He had stocked canned goods and some basics in the freezer.

"Who doesn't?" she asked and rewarded him with a bright smile. She stood and shook out her legs, as if they had fallen asleep while tucked under her. "Let me help."

"Why don't you have a seat at the kitchen table and keep me company. I got the cooking."

Caitlin tilted her head and her gaze narrowed, apparently suspicious of his motives. Then she shrugged. "Okay."

Austin made a fresh pot of coffee, content that they seemed to be on the same page for now. And relieved he could keep an eye on her. He set a mug on the table. He grabbed the sugar and half and half and placed it in front of her. He turned to busy himself with making breakfast, happy to have something to do while he told her more about Christopher Rutherford and what he meant to him. She deserved that much if he expected her to upend her life—albeit temporarily. And it wasn't exactly his fault that she had landed in the crosshairs of a couple of disgruntled locals.

"The missing kid, Chris Rutherford, is like a brother to me." He tossed a piece of bacon on the hot frying pan and turned to glance at Caitlin. She had paused, mid-stir of her coffee, cocking her head. A hint of dark makeup was smudged under her eyes. He barely knew this woman, yet their interactions felt more intimate than they had a right to be.

A million questions flashed across her pretty features, but she remained silent. He turned his back to her to peel another piece of bacon from the slab and toss it in the pan. Easier to tell his story if he didn't have to watch her expression change with each revelation. He didn't want her sympathy, he just needed her understanding. Her cooperation.

"Chris joined the army because he looked up to me. He's quite a bit younger, and I had spent a lot of time at his house because I dated his sister." The bacon sizzled and popped in the cast iron pan. "When he left the army, he felt lost. I think he was looking for a group to join."

"You feel responsible for him." The sympathy in Caitlin's voice made him glad he had his back to her.

"I do. I should have been more honest. Told him about the struggles of being in the army." He shrugged. "Now I just want to find him. Make sure he's safe." Or—the ever-present knot in his gut twisted—let Janelle and his mother know what happened to him once and for all.

"Have you asked Elmer if he recognized him?" Caitlin asked.

"No, I never showed him a photo. I was afraid it would spook him. But I asked him about the guys who work there. In general terms. He claimed there were a lot of short-timers." Austin grabbed a set of tongs and flipped the bacon. "I had hoped to gain access and look around myself. Ask more questions."

"Have you ever asked Elmer about the sheriff?" Caitlin asked. "The kid must have an opinion. He's been in trouble with the sheriff's department more than once."

Austin faced Caitlin. "Elmer's cocky. He implied he was safe at the compound."

Caitlin tucked a strand of hair behind her ear. "Wanda mentioned Wheeler and the sheriff are friendly. Not sure how close they are." She took a long sip of her coffee as if considering something. The bacon sizzled and popped behind him. "The sheriff always rubbed me the wrong way, but I suspected it had to do with his reluctance to hire a woman into the department. I've always felt like I've had to prove myself to him."

Austin spun back around and plated the bacon on a thin layer of paper towels. He scrambled up some eggs, made toast, then slid into the seat next to Caitlin. "I don't have solid proof of any of this. Not yet. I've been working my way onto the compound."

"Yesterday was the first time you gained access?"

Austin nodded. "I let Elmer do some target practice with one of my guns. An hour later, I'm in the compound."

Caitlin poked her scrambled eggs with her fork, but didn't take a bite.

"Didn't I cook them to your satisfaction?" he teased.

"No, that's not it." She set her fork down and met his gaze. "Trafficking in guns is a pretty risky proposition. The FBI is okay with that?"

Austin diverted his gaze and focused all his attention on squeezing out a dollop of ketchup onto his scrambled eggs. "Gotta do what we have to do," he said, trying to act nonchalant. He made a decision right then and there to hope Caitlin was a forgiving person because he'd need her forgiveness once she learned the whole truth.

CHAPTER 25

Later that evening, as the winter darkness gathered before most people even ate dinner, Austin nursed a beer at the local bar, hoping to find Elmer. If he fell off the radar for too long—along with Caitlin's disappearance—people might start to connect the dots and grow suspicious. He had convinced Caitlin to stay up at his bugout cabin, at least for another night, while he continued his investigation. It made him anxious to leave her alone, but unlike her house, no one knew where she was. And she was armed.

The small, dark bar was rather depressing. Someone had strung some white twinkling lights behind the bar—a few Christmases ago, if Austin were to guess, based on the number of dimmed bulbs. Despite the gloomy setting, this location had been a gold mine of information. Many current and former Amish met here after their shifts ended at the nearby cheese factory.

Old habits die hard, and Austin was rewarded a few sips into his first beer. He watched surreptitiously as Elmer strolled in and greeted his friends. He eventually made his way to the bar to order a drink. Austin had never seen him order for anyone but himself. Perhaps he hadn't made that much money at the compound, or maybe the kid was lacking in generosity.

Austin tipped his head but tried to act casual when Elmer noticed him. He drew in a breath, trying to keep his anger at bay. What would he and Solomon have done to Caitlin if he hadn't been there to intervene?

Austin returned to his beer, not wanting to seem too eager to speak to the kid. Elmer casually straddled the barstool next to him. Austin lifted his beer in a faux salute. "Hey there."

"Hey." Elmer seemed dejected. "Did you hear the news?"

Austin frowned and shook his head.

Elmer leaned in conspiratorially. "That jerk Solomon wanted to harass Deputy Flagler last night."

Austin straightened on his stool and narrowed his gaze. "What are you talking about? Is she okay?" He studied the kid's face. "You're gonna draw a lot of heat."

"I tried to stop him, but he was freaked out of his mind." Elmer took a long pull of his beer and glanced around the bar, his eyes wide and fearful. "We made it in, but had to bolt when the sirens started."

Austin planted both hands on the smooth wood of the bar on either side of his drink. "You guys are playing with fire. What about the deputy?" He scrubbed his hand across his beard.

"She was gone." Elmer's eyebrow twitched. "Gone!"

"Wheeler must be angry."

"Are you kidding me?" Elmer almost sounded desperate. "Wheeler's gonna have my head. Solomon is out of control."

"Wheeler's mad because the deputy wasn't home or because you tried to mess with her?"

Alarm widened Elmer's eyes. "Shut up, man, someone might hear you."

Austin lowered his voice. "Hey man, it might not be a good time for me to be dealing with the compound." *The guns.* "That deputy was up there yesterday. People might put two and two together." Austin fought to keep his expression bland and not show the disgust he felt for the kid. What if he hadn't been there to save Caitlin?

Save her? Deputy Caitlin Flagler might very well have been able to handle herself, but he already felt protective of her. Did he somehow feel responsible? Like he had for Chris? Young, impressionable Chris who went into the military because he looked up to Austin. He had encouraged him to enlist. And he had given him tough love when he considered quitting.

Elmer scratched his head roughly, like a dog with fleas. "You can't just walk away like that. Not if Wheeler wants something."

"Does he?"

"He wants to see you tomorrow."

Austin decided in that moment that he had to take a chance. Time was running out. He glanced around. No one was within ten feet, and no one was paying any attention to them. "I need to ask you a few questions and I need you to keep your mouth shut because I think we both know what happens to young men in Wheeler's circle when they don't follow the rules."

Elmer shook his head adamantly. He knew. He knew all too well.

"We both know Aaron Miller didn't die in a hunting accident."

Elmer watched him from under his unevenly cut bangs, making Austin wonder if he gave the kid a few bucks, he'd use it to get a decent haircut. Austin ran his hand over his bushy beard and decided he was hardly one to talk. He scratched his neck, eager to be rid of his facial hair.

Elmer didn't respond. Austin slid his cell phone out of his back pocket, found a photo of Chris and glanced around, making sure no one had tuned into their exchange. "You see this kid around the compound?"

Elmer had lifted his chin, a denial forming on his lips, when Austin stood with the pretense of putting his phone away, but instead using his height and brawn to intimidate the kid.

"Before you say something you regret, if you lie to me, I'll let the sheriff's department know what you were up to yesterday." He casually leaned an elbow on the bar. "Or maybe I'll go right to Wheeler." Austin suspected the latter would be worse, especially if the man hadn't authorized the break-in.

"Come on, man, I thought we were friends." Elmer's tone grew whiny. "I made an introduction."

"True. And I bailed you out of jail. I'll leave it up to you to decide who owes who."

"Show me…"

Austin angled the phone's screen toward Elmer. "Do you recognize him?

"How do you know him?"

"A friend. What happened to him?"

Elmer frowned. "He might look familiar. Lots of people come and go. I don't know." His voice lacked conviction. "Solomon might know."

"Why Solomon?"

"Because Solomon takes care of all the problems."

CHAPTER 26

Caitlin couldn't remember the last time she had absolutely nothing to do all day and nowhere to go to do it. The only thing they did was run to Fredonia and pick up clean clothes and toiletries. So, after her shower, she returned to her book, cuddled up with the quilt on the couch, but was too tired to read. She wasn't sure if it was her hunger pangs or the sound of a vehicle approaching that woke her out of an early evening nap. The cabin was cast in heavy shadows.

The engine cut off, the door opened, closed, footsteps sounded on the gravel. Unease gathered at the nape of her neck and her breath came out in a whoosh. She sat motionless under the quilt. Her hand moved over the arm of the couch. She had tucked her gun into the drawer in the side table.

She was confident that she could protect herself. If she had to.

A jangling sounded at the door, a key sliding into the lock. She held her breath until she saw the distinct outline of

Austin standing in the doorway, backlit by moonlight and snow.

"What are you doing here in the dark?"

She shifted toward the edge of the couch and the quilt slid off her shoulders, making an icy chill skitter up her spine. She slapped shut the book on her lap, stopping it from tumbling to the floor. She stretched out her legs. Austin stepped into the room and turned on the light. Caitlin held up her hand. "Ugh, so bright."

A hint of a smile whispered across his handsome face. He lifted a bag. "I brought takeout. Do you like Chinese?"

How did he know? Her stomach growled. "Food!" She jumped up and tossed the quilt on the couch behind her. Her hunger allowed her to forget the chill in the air. She grabbed the bag from him and carried it over to the table. She undid the cover on the white container and breathed in deeply. "Oh, beef and broccoli. Yum." She turned, suddenly aware that he hadn't said anything.

He was standing there, watching her. "I took a chance. It was either Chinese or sandwiches from the diner. You didn't answer your phone."

"Oh, I must have dozed off. Sandwiches would have been fine, but I love Chinese food." She rushed over to the cabinet and grabbed two plain white plates. She flipped them over in her hands. "Should I wash these?"

"No, I was up here recently. The dust has been blown off everything."

They both dished out food and sat down at the small kitchen table across from one another.

"I'm sorry I left you alone. I didn't know how long I'd be gone."

"Has it only been one day?" She laughed. "I forgot what it was like to have hours on my own without a TV and spotty

Wi-Fi." She wasn't much for wasting time on her smartphone, anyway.

He jerked his chin toward the couch. "Find anything good to read?"

"Yes, a solid mystery. Have you read any of the books here?"

"No, I haven't had time. You'll have to make recommendations."

"Do we plan on holing up here for long?" She laughed, reaching for a fortune cookie, and unwrapped it from its cellophane wrapper. She broke the cookie in half and pulled out a small strip of paper.

"What does it say?" Austin asked, grabbing one for himself.

"Do not trust a man you just met." She glanced up and felt a smile pulling at her lips at the quirk in his eyebrows. She flicked her gaze down to his strong hands cracking open his cookie. "What does yours say?"

Austin made a show of lowering his chin, but not taking his eyes from hers. "A beautiful and smart woman will be coming into your life."

Caitlin dragged a hand through her messy hair. "Ha."

Austin pushed back in his chair. "Sorry, didn't mean to make you feel uncomfortable." He grimaced.

"You didn't. I'm used to ignoring comments from strange men."

Austin scrubbed at his beard. "I can imagine. Ugh…"

"What's wrong?"

"This beard has gotten so itchy."

"You do look a bit like Grizzly Adams."

Austin laughed. "That's a dated reference."

"Call me old-school. Why do you have it, anyway, if it bothers you so much?"

Austin smoothed his hand over it. "I thought it would

make me appear more…official when trying to get into the compound. Like someone who wants to live off the grid."

Caitlin took a bite of her beef and smiled. "Oh, this is so yummy. I was supposed to bring Chinese food to Wanda's tonight."

"You're good friends?"

"She's like a mother to me," Caitlin said around a mouthful of food. "I've known her since I was a little girl." She left out the part about calling dispatch in the middle of the night, afraid. "What took you so long in town?"

"I came up with a new plan."

"Oh yeah?"

"Elmer's in over his head with the compound and with Solomon. He might be willing to cooperate with us."

Caitlin wiped her lips with a napkin. "That might be a risk. Elmer's trouble."

"I think he's looking for a way out. A way to redeem himself."

"Hmmm…" Caitlin said noncommittally as Austin rubbed his neck.

After they finished eating, Caitlin hustled to the bathroom. She grabbed the razor and shaving cream she had picked up at the store today. She snagged a clean towel out of the small linen closet.

Austin narrowed his gaze. "What are you going to do?"

She held up the pink razor and giggled. "What does it look like?"

CHAPTER 27

Austin felt compelled to sit in the kitchen chair Caitlin had pulled out for him.

She patted his shoulder. "Take off your sweatshirt."

He peeled off his sweatshirt and tossed it on the table. The cool air of the cabin chilled his bare arms in his T-shirt. He watched as Caitlin sprayed a dollop of shaving cream into her palms. He reached up and touched her wrist. "Wait, you're not going to shave off my beard." But he didn't want to move. He relished her standing this close to him. He enjoyed the smell of her fragrance, a hint of lavender and cucumber.

Caitlin cupped his bearded chin and seemed to be inspecting him. "How about a trim? No rule about cleaning this up, is there? Won't make you less of a wannabe doomsday prepper, will it?" She rubbed her hands together to lather up the foam.

How could he tell her no? "I suppose you're right. Just don't make it too neat."

Caitlin draped the towel over his shoulders and lathered up his neck. She leaned in close and he had to focus on the scratching sound of the pink razor on his skin. He couldn't remember the last time a woman had touched him so gently, even if it was to shave him.

She worked quietly. When she was done, she took the towel and wiped the shaving cream from his neck. Then she took a pair of scissors and trimmed his beard. He ran his hand across his smooth neck. Caitlin slipped into the bathroom and came out with a mirror and held it up for him. He smiled at her. "I can almost see my old self. Thank you."

Caitlin threaded the towel through her hands and sat down on a kitchen chair across from him. "Tell me more about your 'old self.'"

Austin leaned forward, resting his forearms on his thighs. "My mom died three months ago." He wasn't sure why he was so quick to share this bit of personal information.

"I'm sorry." She folded her hands in her lap and her cheeks grew red. "My mom died when I was eighteen."

"That's tough." Austin studied her face, and she looked like she wanted to say more, but she didn't, so he continued. "That's how I heard about my old neighbor, Christopher. I dated his sister in high school. Chris was always hanging around. You know how little brothers are?"

"I don't. I was an only child." There was something sad in Caitlin's tone, then she brightened. "But I can imagine. So you knew Chris well."

"He looked up to me. It was because of me he enlisted in the army." Austin shrugged. "I might have oversold it, when in reality I think I was trying to sell myself to Janelle. She had graduated from college and had enrolled in grad school. I wanted her to know I had lots of options by following the military path right after undergrad." He held out his hands, feeling a little sheepish.

"Several of my fellow deputies are former military. Upstanding men. Great opportunities."

Austin scrubbed a hand over his beard, surprised by the smooth feel of it. "Of course. The military made me the man I am today. However, Chris got injured during training. When he came home, he was lost. He could have gone back, but he seemed to lose the taste for it. Janelle said he was searching for something. He eventually found it."

"At the compound."

Austin nodded. "Chris met up with the preppers. It seemed right up his alley. Guns. Self-sufficiency. But he quickly became disillusioned. According to his sister."

Caitlin shivered and reached behind her and grabbed his sweatshirt. "Mind if I..."

"Go ahead." He watched as she stuffed her arms into his sweatshirt and lifted it over her head.

"He told his sister the compound was trafficking in drugs. Maybe marijuana."

Caitlin pulled his sweatshirt down over her hips and wrapped her arms around her midsection.

"Janelle told me he thought someone in the sheriff's department was involved. Figured he couldn't get in trouble and would just make some cash in the meantime." He leaned back in the chair and crossed his arms. "You think your boss is capable of taking bribes?"

Caitlin pulled the sleeves of his sweatshirt down over her hands. "I hate to say it, but I wouldn't put it past him." She studied him thoughtfully for a minute. "Tell me, how did the FBI get involved?"

"His sister Janelle came to me." Austin kept his answer short.

A delicate line creased her smooth forehead. "Didn't they consider it a conflict of interest? I mean, for you to be assigned to the case, considering you're personally involved."

He cleared his throat. "FBI's swamped. The world is on fire right now."

"It's scary," Caitlin said, noncommittally. "It doesn't help that we're law enforcement. We always see the worst of the worst." She sighed heavily. "Do you really think Elmer will work with you? I have a long history with him. You can't trust him." He was relieved she had changed the subject.

"He's not an upstanding citizen, that's for sure. But I think he's afraid of what Solomon might do. I can use it to our advantage." *If* he could get her to work with him.

Caitlin held up her hands. "You must realize I won't stay here in the cabin while you figure this all out, right? I'm not a damsel in distress. What kind of deputy would I be if I didn't show my strength?"

Austin pushed his protective feelings aside. He had no right to feel this way. He had no right to expect Caitlin—a woman who barely knew him—to do what he needed her to do. This was his investigation.

"I can do some digging," Caitlin offered. "We can work together."

"I don't want you to get in trouble with your job."

Her bright eyes flashed with a mix of intelligence and excitement. "We can talk to Wanda more. She'll have more insight into the sheriff. She might have information she doesn't realize she has."

"I've been watching that relationship from a distance."

A thin line creased between her eyebrows. "You really have been digging up a lot of dirt since you've been here." She bit her bottom lip, considering. "And Drew and Olivia. Your getting an invitation to their place for dinner was no accident."

"A fortuitous coincidence." Austin smiled. "I went to the lumberyard for supplies and met Drew. When he told me his wife was a deputy, I made sure I got an invitation. I wanted to get close to someone in the sheriff's department. See how far the deception went."

"Is that why you got close to me?" The light in her eyes suggested she was toying with him. "To see if I could be trusted?"

Austin braced his forearms on his thighs and drew her hands into his. They felt small, soft and warm. "If you remember, you barged into my life in the middle of the night when I was minding my own business. Pointed your weapon at me."

Caitlin tilted her head. "Just doing my job." A slow smile tipped the corners of her pink mouth. "So, have you decided if I can be trusted?"

Austin leaned back and ran a hand over his smooth beard. "The jury is still out."

Caitlin rolled her eyes. "You'll never find a more trustworthy deputy. I'm always truthful and I despise liars." She folded the cuffs back on his sweatshirt she was wearing. "So just remember that when you're deliberating."

"I will." He quietly laughed even as the weight of her words hit him. How would she react when she learned he had been lying to her all along?

CHAPTER 28

Caitlin watched as Austin leaned back in his chair and concern clouded his brown eyes.

"Hey, I was just teasing you," she said, leaning forward and playfully swatting his thigh. She did consider herself to be trustworthy, but she couldn't figure out why her comment had elicited such a look of concern. "You suddenly look like you have the weight of the world on your shoulders."

Austin blinked and caught her hand. His thumb brushed across the inside of her wrist, sending waves of attraction rushing up her arm. Caitlin couldn't remember the last time she had felt this way. The few times she opened up her heart —to feel romantic attraction—it always died a spectacular death.

She had witnessed her mother in one disastrous relationship after another. Why should she expect anything different? Especially after meeting someone under these bizarre circumstances.

She slowly pulled her hands away and tucked them under her armpits to keep them warm from the sudden coolness. A flash of confusion swept across his face, then disappeared.

She squared her shoulders and smiled tightly, trying to dismiss the embarrassment making her hyperaware. "Perhaps we should keep this on professional terms." Just as the words slipped out of her mouth, she felt silly. He hadn't proposed marriage or anything. They were just warming up to each other. But she wasn't the kind of woman to allow herself to get physically close if they weren't in a solid relationship.

She dipped her head and dragged her hand through her hair, tugging on a few knotted curls. How had she landed in this spot?

"That's probably best." Austin's deep voice vibrated through her. The sincerity in his tone made her almost sorry for drawing the proverbial line in the sand. She lowered her gaze to the orange swirl in the old linoleum flooring. She believed he meant it and couldn't deny the hint of disappointment dampening her mood. Man, she was messed up when it came to men.

Austin cleared his throat, bringing her attention to his warm gaze. He leaned forward and seemed to consider something. When he finally did speak, it wasn't what she had expected. "You're right. We should reach out to Wanda. We need to find out what she knows."

"She wouldn't be involved." A pool of icy dread gathered in her stomach. Her beloved Wanda loved to chat, which made her very good at her job as a dispatcher. She was able to draw information out of people, sometimes getting them to reveal things they might otherwise not. She tried to think back on exactly what she had said to Wanda this morning. "She's never betrayed a confidence." Her voice unexpectedly cracked.

He tilted his head in curiosity. "Not intentionally."

"How should we handle it?"

"I don't want to put her in jeopardy," Austin said. "We should talk to her in person and assess the situation."

"Okay…"

"Call her now. Set up a meeting." Austin ran a hand over his beard and a funny feeling swirled in her belly when she thought about standing close to him, touching him, smelling his clean scent while she shaved him. "How about breakfast? That won't sound any alarm bells, will it? It needs to be outside Hunters Ridge."

Caitlin nodded enthusiastically. "A few times a year we meet at this cute little diner outside Fredonia that has the best desserts." She held up her hand before he questioned the practicality of that. "Yes, we have dessert after breakfast."

"Call her and don't forget to tell her not to say anything to the sheriff in the meantime."

CHAPTER 29

The next morning, Austin sat across from Caitlin at the diner not far from Fredonia. Caitlin fidgeted with her hair as she held her cell phone to her ear. She worked her lower lip. After a few beats, she tossed it down, and winced as it clattered and skittered across the smooth Formica.

Austin stopped the phone's forward momentum, saving it from crashing to the floor. He palmed it and handed it over to her. "Still no answer?"

"No. Wanda is never late." She lifted her eyes and something akin to fear flittered in their depths.

He reached across the table and brushed her fingertips slightly, needing to comfort her. A feeling he didn't quite understand, considering he had only met her a few days ago. Maybe he had found something in her he had been missing since before his mother died. Their gazes connected, and she gave a subtle shake of her head, as if thinking better of it, and abruptly pulled her hand back. A soft pink infused her cheeks, and she lifted her coffee mug and took a sip.

At that exact moment the server appeared again, probably

a student from the local state college. She looped her thumbs into her green apron and rolled up on the balls of her feet in her comfy sneakers. "You guys ready to order?"

"Um…" Caitlin looked at him, then held out her hand. "Go ahead." She fumbled with the plastic menu, as if she needed another minute to decide although they had been here for thirty minutes, waiting for Wanda Reynolds to arrive. He had already checked in with Elmer and he didn't yet have a time for the meeting with Wheeler at the compound. Austin felt like this case was about to break wide-open or fall completely apart. The last thing he needed was the coffee he had just downed.

Tamping down his own spiraling thoughts, Austin slipped the menu from Caitlin's hands and closed it. "I'm sorry. We won't be eating."

The server jerked her head back, a bit confused, but her expression remained bland. "No prob." She tore off the receipt from her pad and slid it on the table. "You can pay for your coffee at the register." She held out her hand. "Take your time." She rolled her eyes as if to say the place wasn't very busy anyway. "Have a good one." The young woman spun on her heels and strolled away, resuming a conversation with a young man busing a nearby table. Caitlin had followed her movements, too.

"Remember being that age?" she asked.

He smiled. "When you think you know everything, but you know nothing at all?"

"Or maybe you know too much." Her eyes pulled away from the young couple and landed on him again. There was so much about her he didn't know. She placed her hand flat on the table where the menu had been. "Aren't you hungry?"

Austin shook his head and drank the last bit of his coffee. He was, but that was secondary. "Let's go to Wanda's house. Make sure she's okay."

Caitlin frowned. "Do you really think something happened to her?"

"Just a precaution." The words fell from his mouth. The need to reassure her was strong.

She slid out of the booth and stuffed her arms into her bulky winter coat that had been on the seat next to her. Austin tossed down a tip large enough to make up for occupying a table and not ordering breakfast. He paid for the coffees at the register and held the door open for Caitlin. The scent of his shampoo on her made him smile, but he shook the distracting thoughts aside.

Once they were both in the cab of his truck, he reached out and covered her hand. This time she didn't pull away. "Keep trying Wanda. Maybe her phone battery is dead, or she had car trouble. If she answers, we can meet someplace close to town."

"The point of meeting here was so that we wouldn't run into anyone we know."

"We'll figure it out."

"Yeah…" Caitlin said, noncommittally, releasing a shaky breath.

Austin squeezed her hand, then pulled it away. "We'll be at her house in forty-five minutes…" He pushed his foot on the accelerator. "Or less."

He was rewarded with a half-smile. "Thanks."

Austin checked all his mirrors and his blind spot before pulling out and around the slower-moving vehicle in front of him. Tension hung heavy in the small space.

Caitlin glanced over at him, then turned back toward the window, covering her mouth loosely with her hand as she seemed to be fidgeting. "The first time I ever talked to Wanda was when I was about ten. I had called 911."

He was searching for the right words, the right question, when Caitlin continued.

"My mom would leave me alone a lot at night. I dialed 911 when I thought I heard someone breaking in." She sniffed.

"Was there?" Who would leave a child alone at night?

"No, just the active imagination of a little girl." Caitlin shifted in her seat. "Wanda gave me her cell phone number so I could call her whenever I wanted." She shrugged, a barely perceptible gesture under her thick coat.

He tried to imagine a young Caitlin, home alone, talking on the phone to a kindly dispatcher. He cleared his throat. "It was just you and your mom, then?"

"Yeah, my dad was never in the picture. My mom would be out at the bar. Or at some guy's." Caitlin turned her head toward the passenger window. "Wanda was the one who came to my house to tell me." She sniffed. "My mom hit a tree after a night of drinking. That's how she died."

Austin gasped. "That's awful. Oh man, I'm sorry."

"Me, too." There was a faraway quality to her voice. "She picked men and drinking over me. Always." She fidgeted in her seat and tugged on her seat belt, as if she had been embarrassed by sharing something that made her vulnerable. "Wanda has always been there for me. She's one of the few people I trust." She sighed. "It's been a long time since I've told anyone." She lifted her shoulders, then let them fall. "I haven't had to." She played with the cuffs of her winter coat. "Everyone that has lived in Hunters Ridge has already known about my past."

"I know a bit about what it's like to grow up in a community where everyone knows you," Austin said, searching for common ground.

"You said you grew up in Buffalo."

He nodded. "Buffalo is like a small town, especially when your parents live in the same house for forty years." He laughed. "Everyone knew what little Austin was up to. I couldn't get into a tussle with the neighbor kid or skip school without a watchful neighbor calling my mom."

"Sounds idyllic."

Austin cut her a sideways glance. "It was, I just didn't realize it at the time." He ran a hand across his soft beard. He stared out the windshield and read the quaint *Welcome to Hunters Ridge* sign with a black silhouette of a horse and buggy.

"Turn here. Wanda lives about a mile up," Caitlin said.

Austin waited for a horse and buggy approaching from the other direction, then turned. Caitlin pointed to a well-tended home set back off the street. The gravel driveway had been cleared of snow. Austin pulled up alongside the house, and Caitlin reached for the latch.

She opened the door a fraction, then twisted to look at him. Fear radiated from her wide eyes. "Something's not right."

CHAPTER 30

Caitlin gripped the cool handle of the passenger door on Austin's truck and found herself frozen in place. An eerie feeling swept over her. One of those "before" moments etched in time. She had that same icy pool of apprehension knotting her stomach the night her mother never came home. A subtle memory pushed into her consciousness: Wanda holding her hand as they walked down the cold, stark corridor leading to the morgue in the basement to identify her mother's body. Wanda had offered to do it for her, but Caitlin had to do it herself. She thought it would bring closure; otherwise she might forever be waiting for her mother to return home from yet another night out.

Instead, her mother's gray skin, her waxy lips... No closure. Only nightmares.

"Caitlin?" The question in Austin's voice had her blinking, and she momentarily snapped out of it. She slid out of the passenger seat and pulled her unzipped jacket in around her. She tuned into Austin climbing out of his side. His footsteps grew closer, and she realized in that moment how quickly she had grown accustomed to his presence. His strength. And even if she didn't want to admit it, his protective nature.

"The door's ajar." Caitlin moved forward on shaky legs. *What's wrong with me? I've approached strange houses in the middle of the night.*

Austin gently placed his hand on her shoulder. "Hold up."

Caitlin's instinct was to protest. To tell him she didn't need a man to protect her. But this was Wanda. The closest thing she had to a mother. She couldn't shake this horrible sense of foreboding. She complied and allowed him to take the lead. She watched as he pulled his gun from a holster on his waist.

He cautiously approached the door and called, "Wanda!"

Caitlin's heartbeat thrummed in her ears. She flexed her hands, aware of her gun in its holster under her coat.

"Stay here while I make sure it's clear," he said.

Caitlin nodded, unable to talk around the lump in her throat. Austin slipped into the house on high alert, the way Caitlin had done hundreds of times in the line of duty, but here she stood helpless.

After a few moments, she heard Austin calling her name. The urgency in his tone sent adrenaline coursing through her veins. "Come quick," he called.

Caitlin burst through the door, passed the entrance to the sunroom with the wailing TV, to the kitchen where she bumped her shoulder on the arched doorway. Her heart dropped to her shoes, and she fell to her knees. "Wanda." Unconscious. Sprawled on the floor. "Is she...?" Her jaw trembled.

Austin gently touched Wanda's neck. She was slumped against the bottom kitchen cabinets, her head tilted awkwardly to one side. Carefully supporting her neck, Austin moved her flat on the kitchen floor. Blood matted her hair.

"Don't move her," Caitlin cautioned.

"I have training. I'll make sure she's okay." Austin pivoted in his crouched position. "Call 911."

Caitlin pushed to her feet. She had left her cell phone in the truck. She scrambled to grab the portable phone from the wall. With singular focus, she dialed the number. Roger, the elderly man who ran dispatch weekday mornings, answered the phone. "I need an ambulance." She gave the address which the man immediately recognized. "Yes, Wanda is injured. I don't know what happened. She's unconscious."

"Caitlin, dear"—the term of endearment from the elderly man on the other side of the line didn't strike her as condescending, coming from him—"the ambulance is on the way." Roger paused, probably realizing everything he was saying would be recorded. "Are you safe?"

Unease suddenly made her sweaty and nauseous at the same time. "Yeah, I'm not alone."

"I'll say a prayer." The man had worked dispatch for as long as Wanda. Maybe longer.

"Thank you." Her voice broke over the second word. "I'm going to end the call." She knew protocol was to stay on the line, but she had Austin here.

"Keep me posted," Roger said. "And Caitlin, Wanda is a tough old broad. She'll be fine."

Calling her dear friend a tough old broad made her bristle, but she bit back a negative reaction. "I will. I will." She ended the call and tossed the handset on the counter with a clatter. She took Wanda's cool hand in her own. "I'm here, Wanda, I'm here."

Austin continued to monitor Wanda's vitals while Caitlin knelt back on her heels, helpless. "Is she going to be okay?"

Austin shot her a sympathetic gaze, but didn't say anything. In the distance, sirens wailed. Austin rose to his feet. And Caitlin scooted closer to Wanda and took her hand in hers. He snapped a few photos of the kitchen and glanced around, apparently assessing the scene from a professional standpoint.

Her nerves felt fried. She inhaled deeply and thought about her conversation with Roger at dispatch, and she mentally sent up a prayer. *Please don't take Wanda from me.* Then realizing how selfish that sounded, she continued in her head, *Please let Wanda be okay. Let her fully recover and let us figure out who hurt her.*

Austin gently touched her shoulder. She wanted nothing more than to stand and let him wrap her in his warm embrace, but she needed to be strong for Wanda.

"I'll go direct the paramedics. You okay?" They locked gazes, and she nodded. A silent tear trailed down her cheek. "I'll be right back," he said.

Caitlin turned her attention back to Wanda. She leaned forward and brushed a strand of hair from the woman's forehead. "I'll make sure I find out who did this to you."

"Caitlin?" Something in Austin's voice made her pivot. She grabbed the back of the chair to steady herself. The sheriff stood in the doorway, taking in the scene. A fresh wave of nausea made her swallow hard.

"Sheriff." Caitlin pulled herself up on the chair. Her legs wobbled. She had been expecting the paramedics, not him, but of course…the sheriff. Her mouth went dry. She dipped her head and swiped at a tear with a shaky hand, trying to get a grip on her emotions. A mix of fear, sadness, rage swirled inside her, but she would not give the sheriff an ounce of satisfaction of seeing her unravel. He had been waiting for that day. An excuse to get rid of one of his lady deputies. Oh, she disliked that expression. She cleared her throat, realizing that her thoughts were irrational. "I found Wanda on the kitchen floor." She glanced around, as if for the first time. "She must have hit her head on the way down.

This doesn't look like she fell." She turned and saw the glass coffeepot shattered in the corner. Had she dropped it or thrown it at her attacker? "There was a struggle."

Something flashed on the sheriff's face, but quickly disappeared. Perhaps everything she was hearing about the sheriff had gotten to her. Had he hurt Wanda for some reason? The question got lodged in her throat. But why?

"Step back," the sheriff said, as if he was first on scene for some random victim in Hunters Ridge, not his coworker... and something more.

The paramedics entered the room, and Caitlin pressed herself against the cabinets in the small space. Joey, the younger of the two paramedics, had gotten first-class training in the military. He set down his arsenal and got to work stabilizing Wanda. A warm flush of dread prickled her skin, and she got light-headed, feeling an out-of-body experience.

She sniffed her emotion, then scooted away from the cabinets. She had to give the medical personnel room to work. Pete, the other EMT, disappeared and a clacking sound preceded Austin and him ushering the gurney into the room.

The kitchen fell into a hushed silence save for the mechanical sounds of equipment and buckles and squeaky wheels as they hoisted her precious friend onto the gurney and wheeled her out of her cozy home.

The sheriff and Austin followed her out. Caitlin slipped back into the kitchen. Wanda's mug sat on the counter filled with coffee, black. She never drank it black. Whoever came in surprised her before she had a chance to add half and half. She kept her rioting emotions at bay and studied the scene with a critical eye. "What happened here, Wanda?"

Cool air swirled into the room. The front door must be propped open. Wanda would grumble, *I'm not paying to heat the neighborhood.* Caitlin blinked slowly and smiled at the thought.

Please, God, let her be okay.

Caitlin did one last glance around the kitchen to determine what might be out of place before she steeled herself and headed outside. She snagged Wanda's house keys from the hook so she could lock up on her way out. The ambulance left with Wanda inside. She turned to find the sheriff talking to Austin.

Caitlin swallowed hard. She pulled the door closed and inserted the key. Austin said something to the sheriff, then called to her, "Meet me in the truck. I'll take you to the hospital."

Caitlin fought with the lock, wondering when Wanda had last used it. Tingles of awareness had her turn to find the sheriff standing a few feet away. "I'll take a look around before you lock up."

Caitlin raised an eyebrow.

The sheriff continued, "Like you said, it looks like an altercation. I need to take care of my employees. Make sure no one thinks they can take advantage of them."

"I...um..." His sincerity threw Caitlin off. Should she be offering him comfort? Had she misread the situation? Had she been too trusting of Austin? Believed the unsubstantiated rumors? She dragged her hand through her hair. She didn't know what to make of all this. Maybe it had just been a break-in. Hunters Ridge wasn't without its crime. Maybe Wanda hadn't been targeted. A dull thumping started behind her eyes.

The sheriff reached out and touched her elbow in a rare show of compassion. "I know how much Wanda means to you." He removed his hand and held out his palm. "I've grown quite fond of her, too." He laughed in a way that grated on her nerves. In her state of mind, she didn't know if it was warranted, but that was how she felt. "We'll find out what happened here. I promise."

She gave him a quick nod—what choice did she have?—then twisted the lock she had recently fought to engage. "Let's take a look."

The sheriff shook his head. "You go to the hospital. I'll check it out."

A knot tightened in her belly. How could she refuse him? "Okay." She hated the uncertainty in the single word. She'd turned to walk away when he called to her.

"When did you get back from your trip to Buffalo?" There was a hint of accusation in his tone. She had told Wanda to lie for her.

"Yeah, um—"

"And how do you know Austin Young?" The sheriff cut her off, sending her off-balance.

How does the sheriff know his name? Is he aware the FBI are investigating the compound even though Austin said he was here without letting local authorities know?

Caitlin's mind raced. She was normally clear and concise in her thinking—or at least she tried to be—but her worry for Wanda clouded her judgment. "We met in town." She forced a lightness to her tone. "I'm surprised you know him."

"You met in town? Or after answering a disturbance call?" His questions made goose bumps race across her skin. He must have reviewed the calls coming into dispatch. But why? As part of his job, probably. She couldn't separate her professional curiosity from her mounting paranoia.

Justified paranoia. With information from a man she had only recently met. The other man could be a jerk, but he was her boss. The sheriff had never crossed the line. Had he?

He tipped his chin, accentuating his jowls. "Do you make a habit of hanging out with men you meet on the job?"

Caitlin knew enough not to push back when her boss had

her in a corner. "No, Sheriff. I don't. That call appeared to be a misunderstanding. Turns out Austin Young is friends with a friend of mine." She decided to leave Olivia's name out of it. No need throwing anyone else under the bus professionally.

Sheriff Littlefield leaned in close and she could smell the coffee on his breath. "Be careful with him. I've heard some sketchy things."

"Really?" She fought to keep her tone even. She knew she shouldn't listen to the sheriff, that he was baiting her, but she hadn't had a strong history with men dating back to the shady men her mother brought home.

The sheriff swiped his finger under his scrunched-up nose. "He was stirring up trouble at the compound." He shifted so that his back was to Austin. "I heard your new friend was trying to traffic in guns."

Caitlin felt the blood draining out of her face. *How does he know?* "I don't believe that. Not Austin." She wondered if she sounded convincing.

The sheriff adjusted his hat. "How well do you know him?"

Caitlin pressed her lips together, not wanting to admit she had only met him the other day.

"Maybe we could use your new friendship to see what he's up to. That would be a nice feather in your cap." He waggled his eyebrows in a way that made her more uncomfortable than usual. "When are you on duty again?"

"Um, a few days." She was frustrated with her stammering.

"Come to my office, say tomorrow. We'll talk." He rolled up on the balls of his feet and rested his arms on his belly. "I did some digging. Your friend is former military. A loner. The type of person who would be drawn to a preppers group." He cleared his throat. "But Wheeler was alarmed when he was offering them guns."

"Like I said, I don't believe he'd do that." She held her gaze steady even as sweat pooled under her arms.

"Maybe you can do some undercover work."

"Okay." She sniffed. "If you don't mind, I'd like to get to the hospital…with Wanda."

"Of course. I'll be right behind you after I look around her place." The simple statement felt like a warning, but once again, she couldn't read past his flat affect.

"I'll keep you posted," Caitlin said.

The sheriff nodded solemnly. "I'd appreciate it." His tone sounded sincere, yet something flickered in the depths of his eyes that sent a flutter of bone-deep fear coursing through her.

She gave a quick tip of her head. The thick emotion in her throat made it impossible to speak.

The sheriff jerked his chin toward Austin. "And be careful."

CHAPTER 31

*A*ustin muttered to himself that he should've hung back before getting into his truck. Caitlin had been right behind him when the sheriff called out to her. Now she and the sheriff seemed deep in conversation, and he had no way of eavesdropping through the closed door.

Austin slung his hand over the steering wheel, acting casual. The last thing he wanted to do was draw attention to himself, not when he was so close to gaining access to the compound. He quickly checked his phone to see if Elmer had called about his next meeting. *No go.*

When the sheriff shifted to look in his direction, Austin lifted his hand to casually shield his face from the man's view. He wanted to be a face in the crowd, but he figured the sheriff would take note of a man who was suddenly in one of his deputies' lives. So much for keeping his and Caitlin's association a secret. That had been the whole reason for him abducting her in the middle of the night. Now the sheriff—and soon Wheeler—would know of their affiliation.

After a few more minutes, Caitlin walked toward his truck. Frustration, disappointment maybe, curved her shoulders slightly. He reached over to push open the passenger door, but her efficient movements beat him to it. A crisp wind swept into the interior of the truck as she climbed in. Her lips twitched as she buckled herself in.

"You all set?" he asked.

"Yes." Something in the single word suggested the emotions she wore on her sleeve were directed at him.

Austin jammed the vehicle into drive. "Hospital?"

"Please." She turned away from him and stared out the window.

"The sheriff went back into Wanda's house."

"Uh-huh...he wanted to look around since her injuries looked suspicious."

"Oh, man," Austin said, not hiding the disbelief from his tone. "Then if they find any evidence implicating him, he can say he was inside investigating." He slammed his fist on the steering wheel.

"That's not our only problem," she said softly, as if still processing her thoughts.

"What?" Austin glanced her way quickly, then back to the road.

"He did some digging into you."

"My identity will hold." His past work with the FBI would see to that.

"And he knows you're trying to sell them guns. Claims Wheeler is alarmed."

"You've got to be kidding me." Anger surged again.

"Oh, it gets better," Caitlin laughed ruefully. "He wants me to keep an eye on you."

"I've got to move fast."

She drummed her fingers on the thigh of her jeans. "This has the potential to blow up my career if this goes sideways." Angst made her slump into her seat.

"The sheriff is up to no good. You've got to trust me on

that. Just the fact that he knows what I'm up to is telling. Someone is feeding him that information. Most likely Wheeler."

Caitlin flipped up her hood and sank into it. She was apparently done discussing it, for now.

Austin wrapped his hands around the steering wheel and his knuckles grew white. "Where's the hospital?"

"Head toward town."

Austin followed her directions and about ten minutes later turned into the hospital parking lot and jammed the gear into park. He shifted in the seat to look at her. "What's on your mind?"

"I don't have the best track record with men. I'm laying a lot on the line by trusting you. If there's anything you're not telling me, you need to tell me now." The pleading look on her face broke something open inside him.

Austin leaned toward her, then got the sense that he was crowding her, and he didn't want her to climb out of the truck and run away. "I am who I said I am." He could hear his pulse rushing in his head.

Caitlin blinked slowly, as if bracing for bad news. "What does that even mean?"

Austin cleared his voice. "I'm working this case on my own."

"What?" The single word came out high-pitched. "You're not really with the FBI?" All the air seemed to go out of her. "You tricked me. Now I'm going to look like a fool. My career…"

"I am FBI. I didn't lie about that. Let me explain," Austin pleaded.

"I think I've heard enough."

CHAPTER 32

A swirl of emotions Caitlin couldn't get a handle on made her feel like she was having an out-of-body experience. She had worked hard to be respected as a deputy. To do a solid job. But now some slick-talking outsider comes in and convinces her he's working with the FBI?

Ugh! What a fool I've been!

Fisting and unfisting her hands, she strode toward the main entrance of the hospital, not waiting for Austin Young...Grayson...whoever he was. She consciously had to relax her jaw, she was so mad. What other half-truths or lies of omission had he told? Had she been as naive as her mother and trusted a handsome face? Had she risked everything for him?

Her cheeks warmed again when she thought of their romantic evening when she had trimmed his beard. She had allowed herself to imagine that maybe, just maybe, this would be the start of something.

You're a fool. Her mother's last angry words bounced in her head. She had tried to stop her mom from going out the night she died, even though her mom wanted to celebrate a new job. Caitlin knew she'd be tempting fate by going to the bar, and instead of convincing her, the pair had gotten into a horrible fight. And that was the last memory she had of her mother.

Her mother's ashen face floated to mind. The one she had identified in the basement of this very hospital. No, her mother yelling at her hadn't been her last memory. Her cold, dead body had.

Caitlin went up to the young security officer at the main desk. "I need to see Wanda Reynolds." She found herself holding her breath, afraid of what the woman would say after she keyed in some information in the computer in front of her.

She looked up. "She's still in the emergency room." She tapped a few more keystrokes. "Are you family?"

"Um—"

The woman picked up on her hesitation. "Only family is allowed in the ER exam rooms."

Caitlin reached into her wallet and pulled out her law enforcement ID.

The woman nodded. "Let me make a phone call." After she hung up, she said, "You can go back soon. The doctors are examining her." She pointed to the waiting room. "They'll send someone out to get you when she's ready."

"Okay, okay..." Caitlin had to do something with this nervous energy. She turned around and came up short. The sympathetic look on Austin's face made something inside her shift. Of course he had followed her in. Despite their disagreement, despite his secrets, she didn't expect he'd simply drive away. She hadn't been that wrong about him, had she? Deep down he was a good person. Right? He'd risked his entire investigation—regardless of how questionable it was—to save her from Solomon and Elmer.

"Are you okay?" He reached out and gently touched her elbow. She could barely feel it through her thick winter coat.

She shook her head, her hair brushing against the faux fur of her hood. "Of course I'm not okay," she bit out, more harshly than she had intended. An elderly couple sitting in the waiting area looked up at them. She didn't want to make a scene, and Austin must have recognized that because he guided her into a quiet corner beyond a piano to another small seating area, but they remained standing.

"I'm sorry I didn't spell everything out for you," Austin said as he scrubbed a hand across his face.

She ignored her annoyance at his choice of words and focused on the clean lines of his beard. She really had done a nice job. The intimacy of that moment had been lost and had been replaced by a coolness she couldn't shake. "You're putting my career on the line by not telling me the whole truth."

Her shoulder brushed against the large window, spotted with dirty snow thrown off by plows clearing the hospital driveway outside. This man's very presence did something to her insides, and she needed to be objective. Not influenced because he was a nice guy, or a guy who played at being a nice guy. Her mother had fallen for her share of so-called "nice guys," and Caitlin refused to be as easily fooled. But hadn't Austin been as bad as the men her mother fell for? He had worked his way into her heart through a different means: by claiming to be assigned to this case by the FBI. By appealing to her strong sense of right and wrong. By making it personal.

She sighed her frustration, then tuned into his face. He seemed to be at war with himself, uncertain what he could say. "Are you really searching for an old friend who went missing after working at the compound?" Caitlin kept glancing toward the doors leading to the emergency room, eager to check on Wanda.

He stared into her eyes for a long moment, then glanced over his shoulder. "Yes, that's why I broke the rules. I am FBI, I didn't lie about that. I took a leave of absence when my mother got sick." He stepped back and leaned on the couch, wrapping his fingers around the fake leather on either side of him. He kept his voice low, forcing her to move toward him. "Mom had taken care of my dad for years. When she fell ill, I thought it was time for one of her kids to step up. My sister is a surgeon in her residency." He bowed his head and rubbed the back of his neck. "Not exactly the best time to take a pause in your career. It was up to me." He seemed to be studying a tile on the floor between them. "I'm glad I did because she got sicker quickly and died." He drew in a deep breath. "When Janelle told me Chris was missing, I went to my supervisor. He told me they'd do what they could, but I knew right then and there it wouldn't be a priority. That's when I extended my leave and worked the case on my own. Outside the FBI."

Caitlin's gaze shifted to the cluster of chairs, and the elderly couple had disappeared. Now a woman sat alone, apparently engrossed in her phone. The security guard had stood and was messing with a printer behind her desk. This conversation was as private as it was going to get in a public venue. "And the sheriff? Is what you told me about him true? Or was that your way of keeping me from reporting back to him?" Even as she asked, she couldn't believe Austin would be that duplicitous. She held her breath. Could he have been?

No. No. No. A ticking resumed in her head. How many times had Sheriff Littlefield dismissed her when she pointed out a concern in the community that didn't fit into what he wanted to hear? Was he carefully steering her and her fellow deputies away from the compound? What if some of her peers were also taking payoffs? Caitlin pressed a hand to her midsection, suddenly feeling sick.

"I believe the reports about him are true. The depths of his involvement are unclear, therefore I can't risk any information you or I might share with him going back to Wheeler."

"But now he knows we're friends," Caitlin said, working out how this might affect his investigation. Apprehension warmed her skin. Was there still an investigation? She scratched the back of her head roughly, not caring how it made her look. She was beyond frustrated. "What if Wanda got injured because of something I told her?" The reality of that made her shudder from a bone-deep cold. She pressed her fingers to her temples and sighed. This was such a mess. She'd never forgive herself if she'd put Wanda in harm's way. "I really need to see her."

She glanced toward the ER entrance again, and as if willed into existence, a nurse appeared in the doorway. "For Wanda Reynolds?"

"Come with me," Caitlin said to Austin.

When they reached the door, the nurse held up her hand. "I'm sorry. Only one person. We're busy back there."

Austin placed his reassuring hand on the small of her back. "I'll be right here," he said quietly, close to her ear. "Text me if you need anything."

"Thanks."

Caitlin followed the nurse back to a small private room in the ER. "She is stable, but she's unconscious. We'll move her to a room as soon as someone from transport arrives."

Caitlin wanted to ask how long they thought she'd be out, but she knew the nurse would be just speculating. She needed reassurance. Not guesses, or feel-good answers.

The nurse let Caitlin enter alone. The small space allowed for one chair, a bed, and minimal medical equipment. But what she couldn't take her eyes off of was Wanda. Poor, sweet, "tell it like it is even if it's tough to hear" Wanda. She had a bandage on her head and a deep bruise was already forming on her cheek. She picked up her friend's hand, careful not to disturb the IV.

"Who did this to you?"

CHAPTER 33

Austin called Elmer right after he and Caitlin got back into his truck in the hospital parking lot. Austin breathed a sigh of relief when his Amish acquaintance muttered a gruff hello.

"When does Wheeler want to meet with me?" Austin cut a sideways glance over to Caitlin as she tugged on her seat belt.

"That ain't happening, man. Too much going on." Elmer sounded desperate. "Solomon is unhinged, and I'm not sure I can trust him." Austin recalled how Elmer said Solomon took care of Wheeler's problems. Perhaps Elmer had become a problem.

"Let's meet in person," Austin encouraged.

"I don't know."

Caitlin mouthed the word *Lumberyard?*

Austin gave her a nod. "Can you meet me at the lumberyard in town?"

"Um, okay. Give me about thirty minutes."

"Thirty minutes." Austin ended the call and put the truck in drive. "How'd you know he'd go for the lumberyard?"

"His sister works there. Besides, Drew works there, too,

and won't harass me if I'm lingering and not buying something."

Austin smiled at the spark in her eye. She really loved law enforcement. He hoped he hadn't done anything to jeopardize her career.

From the hospital, the lumberyard was a short drive. It gave them time to get settled before Elmer showed up. Austin gave Drew a casual wave since his new friend was busy with a couple construction workers.

"If I was a betting person, I'd put money on Drew calling Olivia the second he gets back to the office to report that you and I are home-improvement shopping together."

Austin couldn't help but smile. "Would that be that bad?"

Caitlin rolled her eyes. Austin was happy to have "this" Caitlin back, but still felt he was skating on thin ice, waiting to fall through and be frozen out if he moved in the wrong direction.

"I'll ask Drew if we can use the break room to talk to Elmer. It should be private enough," she said, reminding him once again that she had much more on the line than he did.

However, if he wasn't careful, he'd lose his job with the FBI, too.

"I'll wait in the break room so Elmer doesn't bolt the second he sees me," she added.

Austin nodded. "I'll wait for him in the parking lot looking like the scruffy doomsday prepper I'm striving to be." He rubbed his hand over his beard and was rewarded with a half-smile.

Man, he hoped he could salvage this investigation with Elmer. But more than that, he hoped he could win over the pretty redhead who had come into his life at the most inopportune time.

Caitlin entered the break room at the far side of the warehouse that housed stacks of backyard play set kits for children, with fantastic climbing walls and spiral slides. She had seen them pop up in many of the yards around town—Amish and English alike. She remembered the fire that had burned a makeshift trailer-office here a few years back. She hadn't been on duty, but had heard how the owner's son had barely escaped with his life.

She took comfort that some stories had happy endings.

Emboldened that both Drew and the owner Theo knew her, she fixed herself some coffee. While she mixed the sugar and half and half with a weak wooden stirrer at the counter, an Amish woman rushed into the break room and came up short.

Lorianne Graber. Elmer's sister.

The young woman spun around to leave, the fabric of her long dress billowing around her worn boots. Caitlin rushed toward her and stopped short of grabbing her arm. "Lorianne, please, wait."

The young Amish woman slowed, her hand lingering on the doorframe. "I need to go."

"Please." Caitlin stuck her head out of the break room and glanced toward the door. "Is your brother here?"

Lorianne turned around slowly. She had a pleading look on her face. "You need to leave my family alone. My brother has made mistakes, but he's trying to do better."

Caitlin pressed her palms together and centered them on her heart. "Your family has suffered a lot." Lorianne's cherished sister had been murdered in New York City. Elmer's run-ins with the law hadn't helped with the Amish-*Englisch* relationships. "We're trying to help your brother. I think he's in trouble. Real trouble." Maybe Lorianne could convince her brother to trust her. She had a good head on her shoulders.

Lorianne placed a hand on her neck, and a blossom of

pink colored her cheeks. "He's caused so much heartache for our parents."

"My friend is trying to help him. I'll try to help him." The last bit came out before she had a chance to think too much about it. Could she really put aside her dislike for the man to offer him a helping hand?

Lorianne nodded. "Elmer is outside talking to someone. He's been in here before. I thought he had ties to that stupid compound." Lorianne pursed her lips. "They're taking a lot of our youths."

"I know." Caitlin squeezed Lorianne's arm, then let it drop. "Please trust me."

The Amish woman seemed to regard her for a minute, then nodded. Apparently, she realized her family had reached the end of the rope. What did she have to lose? "What do you need me to do?" She sounded defeated.

"Well, right now I need you to go back out there and do whatever it is you do. Don't tell your brother I'm here." Caitlin smiled. "Okay?"

Lorianne sighed heavily. "I had come in here for coffee."

Caitlin laughed. She poured the woman a fresh cup. "How do you take it?"

"Black. *Denki*."

The off-duty deputy handed her new ally a coffee. "Thank *you*."

Lorianne took the coffee and stared at Caitlin for a long minute. "My brother's *gut*. He was just never the same after —" Her face grew pink and she seemed at a loss for words. "They say time heals all wounds, but he's still struggling." Lorianne took a sip of her coffee and grimaced.

"I understand," Caitlin said, "but his past actions have jeopardized others. You realize my job can't allow me to let that go."

Lorianne furrowed her brow under her bonnet. A long

strand of dark hair had escaped her bun and dangled over her shoulder. The young woman had probably thought she'd be married and chasing children by now, but instead she was doing some bookkeeping and other administrative work for Cooper and Sons Lumberyard. The Amish woman seemed to consider something, then said, "He will be judged in *Gott*'s eyes." She sighed heavily and stared down at her coffee.

Caitlin was about to protest, to explain that wasn't how things worked, but decided to show compassion instead. "I'll do what I can." But it didn't mean she'd let him continue to run wild, risking his life and others'. Maybe that would be the kindest thing of all. Help Elmer stop the war going on in his head.

Caitlin pulled out a chair at the small table and sat down with her coffee, trying to appear nonthreatening. She heard their voices before she saw them. Austin allowed Elmer to enter the room first, probably to prevent him from bolting. He had sounded skittish over the speakerphone; he'd jackrabbit, no doubt, upon seeing her. But he had grown to trust Austin.

"Why is she—" Elmer stopped talking the second he laid eyes on her. He shifted from one foot to the other, and plowed his hands through his thick bangs poking out from under his black beanie, which almost made him pass for *Englisch* if it hadn't been for his simple barn coat, brown slacks and standard-issue black boots. Even if he'd tried to run, Austin would have blocked him. Neither she nor Austin were rookies when it came to the skittish.

Elmer wasn't going anywhere.

"Have a seat," Austin said, holding out his hand as if it was a suggestion. It was not.

Caitlin leaned forward, wrapping her hands around her coffee mug. "What do you know about what happened at Wanda Reynolds' house this morning?" They had brought him here to hear what he had to say about Solomon, but something made her ask that question first. His answers would help her decide how much she was committed to helping him.

"Wanda Reynolds," Elmer repeated, his face furrowing. "I don't know anyone by that name."

Caitlin was peripherally aware of Austin moving to stand behind her. It was a reassuring feeling to know someone had her back, completely and entirely. "What do you know about the break-in at my house, then?"

That question elicited a completely different response. He plunked his hands on the table, then dropped them down to his side. He bowed his head and scratched it roughly through his hat.

Caitlin's pulse throbbed in a vein in her forehead. She tamped down her anger and summoned calm. "Come clean now so I can help you."

"Protect you from Solomon," Austin added.

The Amish man shot a nervous gaze up at Austin, then toward the door, before fixing his weary gaze on her. He had dark bags under his eyes. "No one can protect me from him. Not if Wheeler wants me gone."

CHAPTER 34

Austin studied Elmer closely as he leaned back and crossed his arms over his winter coat. His lips twitched, as if he was having an internal battle with his demons.

Austin pulled out a chair across from Elmer and leaned forward, resting his forearms on the table. "We can protect you."

When Elmer refused to talk, Austin said, "I can report to the sheriff that you and Solomon broke into the deputy's cabin."

Elmer's mouth opened and closed. A quiet sound of protest escaped. A defeated man.

"You could go away for a long time. She's law enforcement. The law doesn't look kindly on that," Austin said, watching the kid's face.

That was the tipping point. Elmer pushed back and his chair crashed on the cement floor. Austin and Caitlin jumped to their feet at the same time.

Austin righted the chair with one hand and held his other hand out in a *take it easy* gesture. "Sit down."

Elmer flopped down into it and resumed his arms-across-his-chest stance. He blinked slowly, releasing a breath out of his nose. "Solomon is a jerk."

"So it was his idea to break into my house?" Caitlin asked, remaining standing and on high alert based on her posture.

"*Yah, yah.* It was his. Well…" Elmer's gaze flicked around the room.

"Clyde Wheeler gave him the order?" Austin asked, keeping his voice even.

"You can't go around saying that." Elmer sounded more desperate than before. "He'll never do business with you if he thinks you're saying bad things about him."

Austin studied him closely. Did Elmer still think he was looking to make a deal? Inwardly, he shook his head. The walls of his investigation were closing in. He had to trust his instincts. "I'm going to ask you one last time, and if you're not honest, I'm walking away. You're on your own to handle Wheeler and Solomon." Austin pulled out his cell phone, tapped on the photo of Chris and showed it to Elmer. "You told me Solomon might have taken care of my friend here. I think you know more than you're telling me."

Elmer looked at the image. He quickly schooled his expression, but Austin had caught the emotion that flickered in his eyes.

Austin pressed. "What do you know about my friend Chris? His family is really worried about him." Austin made a show of glancing toward the door leading into the warehouse where Lorianne had disappeared. "Just like your sister is worried about you." He leaned in closer. "Just like you worried about Abby when she moved away to New York City."

At the mention of his murdered sister, Elmer fisted his hands in his lap. "You'll never be able to do anything about it." The Amish man shot Caitlin a furtive glance.

"Why is that?" Austin asked.

"You just can't." Elmer slumped back in his chair. "That's why I'm in it deep. There's no way out."

"Yes, there is," Caitlin said.

Elmer shot her a disdainful look. "What would you know?"

"Is someone in law enforcement tied to the compound, Elmer?"

This time Elmer's eyes widened, and he didn't try to hide his surprise.

Austin reached into an inside coat pocket and pulled out his FBI credentials. A little fib here wouldn't hurt. "I can help." He flipped open his ID and flashed his badge. "I promise."

Elmer dragged a hand through his hair and knocked his winter cap off. "I...I don't understand."

"I've been trying to gain access to the compound to find Chris. His family couldn't get any satisfaction from the sheriff when he went missing."

"The sheriff's not going to do anything."

"He's involved?" Caitlin leaned forward, quietly threading her fingers and placing them on the table.

Elmer looked at Caitlin slyly, then turned to Austin, letting out a long huff. "How can you help me?"

"We can make sure you're safe." At this exact moment, Austin didn't know what that would look like, but he also didn't know what Elmer could deliver. "What are they doing at the compound? Why are they so eager to buy my guns? They're not just preppers, are they?" Austin realized he was putting it all out there. But he also recognized a desperate man.

Elmer shook his head. "Clyde Wheeler is distributing drugs in and out of Canada."

"What kind of drugs?" he asked.

"Marijuana." The inflection in Elmer's voice suggested he wasn't sure. Recreational cannabis was legal across the border and in a growing number of states. It had to be something else, but Austin didn't press.

Austin blinked slowly, then caught Caitlin's gaze. Her laser-like focus was on Elmer. "Is Sheriff Littlefield involved?"

"Um, no, not with the drugs." Elmer spoke with an uncertain tone.

"He's not?" Austin pressed.

"Not exactly." The Amish kid cleared his throat. "But he's paid to look the other way. Make sure the deliveries get through."

"How do you know?" Caitlin asked. Maybe she felt oddly defensive of the sheriff. Or maybe she was angry that her smug boss could betray the badge she so proudly wore.

"I overheard some guys talking." Elmer started muttering, as if realizing what was unfolding in front of him, "Oh man, oh man, oh man. You have to help me. He'll kill me."

"Solomon?" Austin asked, even though he knew the answer. "Just like he killed Chris." He held his breath.

Elmer nodded.

Even though the flicker of hope he had of finding Chris alive had begun to sputter soon after he arrived in Hunters Ridge, this confirmation had all but snuffed it out.

"Chris wanted out." Elmer stared off into the middle distance, as if lost in a memory. "I gave the kid a ride to the Hunters Ridge motel."

"Chris Rutherford?" Austin said, just so he was absolutely clear.

Elmer flashed Austin an annoyed glance, as if to say, *Of course*. He cleared his throat and continued. "When I dropped him off, Solomon was waiting for him."

"Did you see Chris after that?"

Elmer shook his head.

"Did Clyde know he wanted out?"

"You can't get out, don't you see? Not if they don't want you to leave."

"Did Solomon kill Chris Rutherford?"

"I think so." Elmer bit his chapped lip. "I'm in a jam. Wheeler's already asking questions about you and blaming me for bringing you onto the compound." He rubbed his beard roughly. "He's got it in for me. And if he finds out I was talking to Deputy Flagler here, or if they realize you're actually law enforcement, I'm as good as dead."

"Did Clyde authorize that home invasion? At Deputy Flagler's?" Austin could feel Caitlin's gaze on him, but he kept his on Elmer. He didn't want to miss any tells.

"I don't know. I think so. Solomon seems out of control. I mean…sometimes he goes off half-cocked on his own." Elmer shifted in his seat. "Wheeler's goal is to run his operation under the radar. Chris's disappearance didn't cause much of a wave, but he was mad about Aaron Miller."

"Because his family wasn't buying the hunting accident."

Elmer flicked a wary gaze to Caitlin and nodded quickly. "Solomon took him hunting." The statement alone was an indictment.

Austin sighed heavily. These poor guys had no idea what they had gotten involved with, and when they wanted out, Solomon was tasked with shutting them up. Permanently.

Elmer eyed Caitlin suspiciously and palmed his thighs and rocked back and forth. "I should probably take my chances and get out of town." Elmer stared out in the middle distance, as if weighing his options. "Once word gets out that I've spoken to you."

"What kind of life would that be? Stay. Help me take him down," Austin said.

"Even if we get Solomon, who's going to stop the sheriff?"

Elmer's agitation grew. "How many FBI guys do you have working with you? Clyde Wheeler has been training a small army." The resignation in the young man's voice made Austin more convinced that he had to stop Clyde, his operation, his terrorizing of naive young men.

The defeat radiating off Elmer made Austin's nerves hum. He hadn't wanted to expose his position, but he felt he had no choice. Things were escalating. He didn't have the luxury of time.

In the remote possibility that Chris was alive, he had to find him now. And he couldn't leave Elmer exposed.

Austin thought back to his own childhood days, going to Sunday school, and he tried to find common ground with this young man who had once put religion at the forefront of his mind. "Weren't you a fan of David in the Bible?" He couldn't quote book and verse, but everyone knew that story, right? Austin gestured to the three of them sitting at the table. "That's us. We can take out Goliath."

"Do you think Elmer can keep his mouth shut?" Caitlin said as she stood at the doorway leading to the warehouse. She wasn't sure it was wise to let him out of their sight, especially to return to the compound.

"He sure is squirrelly. But if he doesn't show up when they're expecting him, it will raise a lot of red flags." Austin stood and pushed in his chair. The yellow glow of the recessed lights made the skin under his eyes look dark. Perhaps the revelation that Chris was more than likely dead had taken the wind out of his sails.

"I'm sorry about Chris."

Austin pressed his lips together and shook his head. In disappointment, or maybe disgust. "I have to bring him home." He drew in a deep breath and let it out. "One way or another."

"Are you going to call his sister?" Caitlin wasn't sure why the mention of a woman he had once loved tweaked at her heart. Did that make her a small person? Chris's sister was about to get potentially the worst news of her life.

"I'm going to wait until I have answers."

Austin's phone buzzed in his pocket. He fished it out and met Caitlin's gaze briefly before answering it. He put it on speaker so she could hear. "Solomon just called," Elmer said. He was absolutely frantic. "He told me not to bother coming to the compound, that he was coming to me."

"Is that unusual?" Austin asked, holding his phone out in front of him so Caitlin could listen in.

"No, no...." The loud engine roared in the background. She feared his distracted driving would send him into a tree.

The memory of the worst night of her life skittered up her spine. She could imagine Mrs. Graber answering the door to a sheriff's deputy telling her that her son was dead. Just like Wanda had given her the horrible news about her mother.

Austin was saying something, but she had tuned out. She held up her hand and spoke into the phone. "Elmer, is your family home?"

"No, I swung by earlier because I knew they'd be gone. They went to visit my aunt and her new baby."

"Good. Hang up and go straight home. Once you are safely home, call Solomon and tell him you have work to do in the barn. I'll be there before he gets there. I have an idea."

CHAPTER 35

Caitlin ground her teeth. "I don't need you to protect me." The irony of her argument wasn't lost on her. Austin had already saved her in more ways than one, but that wasn't the point. She hadn't gotten this far in her life—mostly on her own—just to turn around and defer to a man. Nope. No way.

"I don't like this idea. Not at all," Austin said as they sped toward the Grabers' farm.

"It's a good plan."

"I don't want you alone."

"I'll be fine. I'll stay out of sight. I need you to head north and alert me if anyone from the compound is headed this way. And I need you to stop the Grabers from returning home. I don't want them to be in danger if they show up while that hothead is there. Solomon is unstable." They'd had enough turmoil in their lives.

"Do you really think Elmer is sophisticated enough to get Solomon to confess?"

"It's worth a try." Caitlin tapped her fingers on the door handle as the trees whizzed by. The heavy snow clung to the pine trees. Her gaze shifted to Austin, and she wondered where they'd both be after this was all over. He'd probably be back in Buffalo, and she'd still be in Hunters Ridge. She had more at stake here. Seeds of doubt about her boss had been sowed; there was no going back.

The Grabers' farm grew closer. "Just pull over on the berm. I'll go on foot up to the barn."

Austin pulled over but kept his gaze straight ahead. The air was thick with tension and she waited a half beat, sensing he wanted to say something. She needed him to trust her, and she had to have full trust in him for this to work. He shifted and met her with an assessing gaze. He patted his pocket in his coat. "Text me the second things go south."

Caitlin shook her head. "Nothing's going south." She raised an eyebrow and felt a smirk pulling at her lips.

"Okay, bad turn of phrase." His Adam's apple bobbed. "Text me if you need backup and I'll text you if you're about to have company."

"Perfect." Caitlin reached for the door.

"Wait." Her eyes dropped to his solid hand on her sleeve, but it wasn't his touch that kept her frozen in place. He lifted his hand to her chin and leaned in. He smelled of outdoors and aftershave. Her stomach did a funny flip.

She leaned closer. Their lips met and her breath caught. His hands slid around to the back of her neck and tangled in her hair. Chills—good chills—raced across her scalp. They deepened the kiss, and she wished more than anything that she didn't have to go.

Alarm fought against the warm and fuzzy feelings. Caitlin brushed her hand across his cheek, and she was the first to pull away. She had to do this.

"Be careful," he whispered in a husky voice.

"I will." She smiled, then slipped out of the truck. A sadness and longing lingered in her gut, mingling with desire. If only they had met under different circumstances. *Ha, if only is the story of my life.*

Caitlin didn't dare turn around, and she quickened her pace as she strode up the Grabers' lane. She took careful steps, not wanting to turn an ankle on the deep ruts from the horses' hooves and buggy wheels. She felt Austin's eyes on her. His lips on hers. His hands...

Stop. Focus. Time was slipping away.

Pinpricks of apprehension washed over her skin. "Go, go, go," she muttered under her breath. They were so close to unraveling something big.

"Hey!" Elmer called to her from across the yard. He was standing in the doorway of his family's home.

Caitlin gestured toward the barn. "Meet me out here." She didn't wait for him to answer. They needed to hurry. She reached the building and slipped inside. She couldn't risk Solomon seeing her on the property. The pigs seemed unaffected by the arrival of an outsider. The smell hit her nose and made her stomach roil. She supposed others grew nose blind to such smells.

She double-checked that her phone was on silent and slipped it into her back pocket, hoping she'd notice the buzz of a text from Austin if the Grabers or someone from the compound was headed this way.

She poked her head out and heaved a sigh of relief when she saw Elmer rushing toward the barn. He was a wild card and she couldn't trust him. He hadn't given her a reason to, but she wanted to give the kid a chance. She understood being the underdog. And second chances. And she wanted more than anything not to cause the Grabers any more pain.

Deputy Caitlin Flagler couldn't give her plan much more thought because Elmer stormed into the barn, his leather-gloved hands flexing and unflexing. He was clearly agitated. "If Solomon finds you here...." He shook his head, then grabbed her shoulder with a surprisingly firm hand and pushed her toward the door. "You need to go."

She shoved his hand away and said, "Don't touch me again."

The young man seemed to be taken aback. His face flushed from anger, or maybe shame.

"Calm down. Keep it together. You've gotten involved with dangerous people. If I go, Solomon is likely to kill you, anyway."

"*Neh, neh*, I can convince him I don't know nothing."

"Tell me, why do you think Aaron Miller is dead and Chris Rutherford has gone missing?" And was most likely dead.

When Elmer didn't immediately answer, she pushed, "Weren't they as smart as you? Maybe just unlucky?" She taunted him and the lines around his mouth relaxed and were replaced by something else. She flicked her gaze toward the barn door. Still no sign of Solomon. She was itchy. She needed to run through the plan before he got here. "I'm going to slip into this first stall and hide. Make sure you bring Solomon fully inside so I can hear you. You need to get him to confess to killing Chris and Aaron. Or at the very least one of them."

"How…" Agitation once again made his breath labored.

"Solomon's smug, right? Use that to your advantage. I have faith in you."

With that, Elmer stopped fidgeting and met her gaze. "You have no reason to."

She nodded. "I do. You're a good man who has made a lot of bad choices. Let's turn this around." The words rang hollow in her ears, but they were necessary.

Before Elmer had a chance to protest, Caitlin's phone vibrated in her back pocket. She slid it out and read the text. Her heart raced. "Okay, he's on his way." The sound of a deep engine confirmed Austin's text. "Turn your cell phone on record and slip it into your pocket." They'd need as much proof as they could get. Caitlin watched him do exactly that, then gave him one more reassuring nod before slipping into the empty stall.

She glanced down, relieved to see that it was clean. However, stepping into a steaming pile right now was the least of her problems. She had to find evidence of Solomon's wrongdoing—and thus tie it to the events at the compound, and her boss—all while making sure Mrs. Graber didn't suffer another tragedy.

CHAPTER 36

*A*ustin didn't like leaving Caitlin on the Grabers' property with Elmer while Solomon was on his way. The first man was in over his head, and the latter one was serious trouble. But Austin had to trust her. She was a trained sheriff's deputy. He scrubbed his hand over his face and pulled his truck into an overgrown lot a couple miles away from the farm. He tucked his vehicle behind some trees. And he waited. He wasn't good at waiting.

But it wasn't long before Solomon raced by in his car. Austin had a visceral response to the man. His gut told him Solomon wasn't the brains of the operation, but he was undoubtedly the brawn. If Elmer could get him to confess, then all things would point back to Clyde Wheeler. And maybe Clyde was the kind of man who would pull everyone down with him—including the sheriff.

Justice for Chris, who Austin feared—more now than ever—was dead.

Austin quickly texted Caitlin to alert her. He drummed his fingers on the steering wheel and the temperature quickly dropped. He could see his breath inside the truck.

His eyes drifted to the clock on the dash. Only ten minutes had passed since he pulled over. He turned his attention back to the road and a horse and buggy came into view. He had to squint to identify the driver and his passenger. His stomach dropped. It was the Grabers. Elmer had told him they were out visiting relatives. Austin muttered and started up his truck. He had to prevent them from going home.

He pulled in behind them. He wasn't sure what he was going to say, but he had to do something. He made sure the quiet country road was empty, and he went around them and gestured to Mr. Graber. The Amish man initially tipped his hat and returned his focus to the road in front of him.

Austin needed to get their attention without spooking the horse. He kept even with the buggy, checking the road ahead of him for oncoming traffic. Thankfully, the wintry roads were empty. Mrs. Graber looked over this time. He couldn't make out her expression under her black bonnet. He waved his hand, suggesting they pull over.

The woman leaned over and said something to her husband, who pulled back on the reins. "Whoa!" The horse came to a stop.

Austin pulled his truck in front of them. He checked his cell phone. No communication from Caitlin. He'd take that as good news.

He hopped out of the truck and waved, rearranging his face into the most aw-gee-shucks-can-you-help-me face. "Sorry to bother you folks." He approached the driver's side of the buggy. He tucked his hands under the armpits of his heavy winter coat. "Mighty cold."

"You didn't stop me to tell me how cold it is."

"No, no sir, I didn't." Austin stalled for time. "Your son's in some trouble."

With the mention of his son, Mr. Graber's face grew tight. "Our son has caused us enough grief. Why are you stopping us on the country road? We're cold and tired. We want to go home."

Mr. Graber was Amish, but it didn't mean he was naive. Austin chose the direct route. "It's not safe."

Caitlin leaned against the cool wood of the empty stall. Elmer scraped the shovel against the metal trough, perhaps feeding the excited pigs. Between the metal on metal and the squealing, she had to strain to hear. She caught a glimpse of Solomon through a narrow crack between the slats. She blinked a few times, trying to get a read on him, but it was challenging at best.

Come on, guys. Give me something I can use.

"What were you doing talking to that deputy in town?" Solomon finally asked, making blood whoosh in Caitlin's head. He knew she had met with Elmer.

"I didn't..." Elmer faltered.

"Don't lie. Someone saw you at the lumberyard." Solomon muttered something Caitlin couldn't make out. "Do you think anything happens without someone blabbing?"

"She cornered me there. What was I supposed to do?" Caitlin figured Elmer was trying to appear indifferent, but the high pitch to his voice made him seem desperate.

"You're not telling her anything, are you?" Solomon's question sounded menacing.

Metal clacked and Caitlin could imagine Elmer tossing the shovel down in frustration. The pigs squealed, then settled down. "What would I tell that deputy? She has it in for me, remember?" Disgust tamped down the nervousness in his voice. "I'm not exactly an innocent around here. Ever since that incident with the fancy people that live on the ridge."

"That's ancient news." Solomon chuckled. "Did they ever figure out you slaughtered the pig and left it on your neighbor's porch last summer?"

"I...um..." Elmer sputtered, and Caitlin found herself fisting her hand. Turned out this conversation revealed things Elmer wished he could have kept secret.

"Oh, come on. Don't act so innocent. Wheeler's going to be hiring you to do his dirty work before long. That was awesome. Proves you got what it takes. Don't mind getting your hands dirty. Unless you turn out to be a wuss."

Caitlin swallowed hard.

"*Neh*, I don't mind doing construction and stuff. It's good money. I ain't gonna do anything else."

"Heck, you want to finally leave this stinking farm forever?" Solomon's voice grew quieter. But Caitlin could pick up a few words. "You can"—*muffled conversation*—"money."

"I don't know," Elmer said. "Like what kind of things?"

Good job, Elmer.

Solomon laughed, an unpleasant sound. "You still buying into the complete story that the Miller kid died in a hunting accident? Fell out of the tree and accidentally shot himself." The guy scoffed. "Yeah, don't be as naive as the rest of them."

"I can't get in trouble," Elmer mumbled.

"Don't worry about that. The money-grubbing sheriff is in Wheeler's pocket. That's why Red is going to find herself in her own accident."

Caitlin rolled her eyes like she hadn't been called "Red" a million times in her life. She angled her head to get a better view. Solomon had his back to her, and Elmer leaned over and picked up the shovel. He planted the blade on the barn floor and leaned on the handle. "She doesn't know anything. That's why she keeps asking. She'll get bored and move on."

Solomon was doing something Caitlin couldn't see. Then

a moment later, he lifted a cigarette to his lips and lit it. He dragged in deeply and exhaled a long cloud of smoke.

"The deputy asked about that *Englisch* kid that was at the compound. I'm sure once he shows up, they'll move on."

Good. He asked about Chris.

"You think they'll find him, huh? You're as dumb as his family." Solomon shifted and blocked her view of Elmer. "That kid thought he was going to be a hero and bring down the operation."

"Marijuana is legal in a lot of places. What's the big deal?" Elmer asked.

"If only it was just weed." Solomon laughed again. He was obviously a man who liked to hold the secrets and dole them out as he saw fit. "Being this close to the Canadian border makes us a perfect location for trafficking in all sorts of illegal substances." Solomon took a step closer to Elmer, and Caitlin quickly ducked back farther into the shadows of her hiding spot.

"You're not going to go running to her now, are you?"

"She's not my friend," Elmer muttered. "I think you're forgetting I broke into her house with you. She needs to keep her mouth shut."

Silence stretched for a beat, save for the wind that whistled through the cracks. Even the animals had grown quiet.

"Wheeler wants to see you." Solomon tipped his head toward the door.

"I got work to do. I'll come up later."

"Nope, now."

"I got stuff to do." Caitlin heard the wobble in Elmer's voice.

"What's up with you? We're leaving now."

Caitlin had to make a quick decision. If she alerted Solomon to her presence, she'd definitely put a target on Elmer's head. She held her breath as the two men left the barn. She crept toward the door. Solomon ducked into his car, and Elmer climbed into the passenger side under his own power. But his body language radiated his reluctance.

Staying out of sight, she muttered, "What are you up to, Solomon?" The engine roared to life and Caitlin pulled out her cell phone and called Austin.

"Are you okay?" Austin asked, concern edging his voice.

"Yes. Come get me. Solomon took Elmer. I'm worried that Solomon might be looking to get rid of another one of Wheeler's problems."

CHAPTER 37

*A*ustin told the Grabers they were free to go home, and he ran back to his truck and raced ahead of them. He found Caitlin pacing at the end of the Grabers' driveway.

She yanked open the passenger door and hopped in. "They went that way."

He listened for the click of her seat belt and took off down the road.

Austin narrowed his gaze as the powerful engine of his truck roared. He flicked a glance in Caitlin's direction. "Where do you think they're going?"

"I don't know, but I don't like it." Caitlin was looking at something on her phone. "I have Google maps open. Solomon's dad has a trailer on a piece of property this way. Used to be a farm before the father got caught up in drugs."

"Where's the father now?" Austin asked.

"Died of a drug overdose two years ago. Sad situation. The kid had to grow up fast." Austin detected a hint of empathy in her tone. "Let's go to the Redman place. It's up here."

Austin rounded the corner with a squeal. A sad-looking trailer sat to the right of a run-down farmhouse. The elements had practically claimed the structure. The roof was covered in moss and caved in. Anyone with any means would have either repaired the roof years ago, or have torn down the place and started anew. Instead, it seemed Mr. Redman had plunked down a trailer and called it home.

Caitlin held up her hand. "Slow up." She pointed toward the back of the property. "Fresh snow tracks. That could be from Solomon's car."

"Okay." Austin drove beyond their lane and pulled over. The gravel crunched under his tires. The plowed snow was piled a couple feet on the edge of the road, providing them with decent cover.

Austin glanced over at Caitlin and saw a look of concentration on her face that was becoming familiar. There was no messing with her. "You go around the front of the property," she said. "I'll go around back. We'll approach the trailer from opposite sides."

He nodded, and they both climbed out of his truck and headed up the lane. She was about thirty feet from the trailer when she stopped suddenly and held up her hand and gestured toward the back. That was when Austin saw them. Solomon and Elmer were near a small rock wall. A well?

His stomach dropped. He tipped his head at Caitlin. "Ready?"

She nodded and they closed the distance between them quickly. Caitlin had her gun out and aimed it at Solomon. "Step away from Elmer."

Solomon slowly turned around, an ugly snarl on his face. Then he turned back to the Amish kid. Without saying anything, he gave him a violent shove. Elmer landed hard on his hip on the small rock wall, all his breath going out of him in a whoosh.

"Freeze!" Caitlin hollered, moving quickly. She forced Solomon down on the ground and cranked one hand then the other behind his back. Austin handed her handcuffs, and she slapped them on.

Meanwhile, Austin helped Elmer to his feet. "You okay?"

Elmer looked shell-shocked. "*Yah*," he finally muttered. He planted his hand on the stone wall and leaned forward. A small spray of pebbles broke free and skittered down the wall of the well into a black hole.

Austin grabbed his arm. "Easy there."

Elmer straightened, his face bloodless. "*Denki*, for saving me. He told me he pushed Chris down here."

"And I would have pushed your sorry butt into the well. Snitches get stitches." Solomon sat in the snow, his handcuffed arms pulled behind him.

"Shut up," Austin said to Solomon, then he turned his attention to Caitlin. Was this how it really ended? Poor Chris in a well. How would he ever tell Janelle?

A memory of ten-year-old Chris coming downstairs with a Monopoly board game tucked under his arm, asking his big sister and her then boyfriend, who had to stay home to keep him company, if they wanted to play. They didn't. They chased him off to bed. The back of Austin's eyes prickled at the memory. If only he could go back in time. Funny how his mind automatically went to the times he blew off the kid and didn't focus on all the hours of playing catch with a football or taking him to pick up his first suit for a junior high dance.

Caitlin pulled out her cell phone.

"Who are you calling? You can't call the sheriff."

"I'm going to call another deputy that I absolutely trust."

They made eye contact and Austin nodded. She had trusted him through all this, and he had to trust her. Besides, it would require too much explaining to his supervisor in the

FBI what he was doing during his leave. That was a consequence he'd face later.

"The deputy can take him to the state police barracks. They'll deal with him outside of the local sheriff's department until we can figure out how far the deceit runs." Then Caitlin turned to Solomon. "The sheriff can't protect you now."

The punk narrowed his eyes. "Who's going to protect you?"

"Shut up," Austin said, "unless you want to add threatening a law enforcement officer to the charges."

Solomon's expression grew smugger. "Such a shame about your friend, Wan-da." He dragged out her name.

"Did you hurt her?" Caitlin asked, raising her voice.

"Too bad I've got no reason to talk. Maybe you should ask Elmer."

Elmer stood back, wide-eyed. He shook his head frantically. "I didn't touch her."

Caitlin wasn't biting. Then her attention was drawn to the approaching patrol car. She introduced Austin to Deputy Dylan Kimble and quickly explained the situation. He readily agreed to take Solomon to a neutral lockup. Perhaps the deputies had already lost faith in their boss for reasons other than the sheriff's suspected involvement with the compound.

The prisoner secure in the back seat, Caitlin patted the hood of the patrol car, indicating that her fellow deputy could head out. Caitlin tucked a strand of hair behind her ear with a shaky hand. Her fair coloring had turned ashen.

"Are you okay?" Austin asked.

She bit her lower lip, then said, "You need to get the FBI involved for real. We have to find out what's going on in the compound once and for all, especially if the sheriff is involved. The investigation has to be done by the feds."

Austin should have felt excited. Instead, dread consumed

him. He was now going to have to explain to his supervisor what he was doing out here on his own. Then he'd have to talk to Janelle, because if Solomon was telling the truth, the kid he taught how to ride a bike was dead at the bottom of the well.

"I'm sorry," Caitlin said as if reading his thoughts. "I had really hoped there would be a different ending for your friend."

"Yeah, me too." His gaze drifted to the well. He pulled out his cell phone. "I have to call this in."

"Um…" Elmer strolled into his line of sight, a meek expression on his face. "Can I…uh…go?"

"No, you are not getting off the hook this time," Caitlin snapped before Austin had a chance to speak up. She jabbed her finger at him. "I will make one last compromise with you. We're going to take you home. You make nice with your parents. That deputy that just left here, he'll pick you up in one hour. If you're not there, or you cause any problems, I promise I will make you regret it."

Elmer shook his head. "I can't go to the sheriff's department. I can't."

Caitlin shifted to look at Austin, who read her mind. "We'll handle that," he said to Elmer who was obviously worried about the sheriff and whoever else might be corrupt within the department. "But like the deputy here said, if you're not where you're supposed to be in one hour, and if you don't cooperate, we'll find you and you might never see the light of day again."

CHAPTER 38

Caitlin let out a breath she hadn't realized she'd been holding when she laid eyes on Wanda Reynolds in her hospital bed. Austin lingered by the door as she went in and touched her warm hand. Wanda's pulse under her fingertips was the reassurance Caitlin so desperately needed. She looked up at Austin, who smiled. She had met him less than a week ago, but felt so much closer than that short time should have afforded.

Austin rolled off the doorframe. "I'll ask a nurse to come in when she has time."

"Thank you." Caitlin lifted a chair and moved it next to the bed silently. She sat down and placed her hand over Wanda's, relief washing over her.

"Wanda woke up earlier today." A kind voice startled Caitlin. She looked up and blinked at the young nurse.

"Really?" She wanted to ask why no one had called her, but she didn't want to appear to be lashing out at the nurse. "She's okay?"

"I was in here when the doctor talked to her. He expects

her to make a full recovery." The nurse smiled and excitement nearly burst from Caitlin's chest.

Austin reappeared at the base of the bed. "Did she have anything to say about what happened to her?"

"No, she said she didn't remember." The nurse rubbed the back of her neck. It was late in the day of what was probably a long shift. "The sheriff had been in here, so I imagine if she had anything to say, she would have told him."

Caitlin shot Austin a quick glance. Then to the nurse, "The sheriff was here?"

"Yeah, for a good chunk of the day. He bolted out of here about thirty minutes ago." The nurse flung her hand in the general direction of the hallway. "Told the nurses not to let anyone into her room. That she needed rest."

"I'm sure she wouldn't mind my being here," Caitlin said, a surge of anger welled in her chest.

The nurse scoffed. "You're fine. We don't take orders from patients' visitors anyway, despite what they think." The young woman glanced at the clock. "Visiting hours do end at eight, so as long as you leave by then it's no problem."

"Thank you," Caitlin and Austin said in unison.

The nurse left and Austin asked Caitlin if she wanted anything. She didn't. She just wanted Wanda to wake up so she could ask her a million questions.

"I need to make a few more phone calls. Are you okay here?"

Caitlin smiled. "Of course."

After he left, Caitlin put her head down on the bed next to Wanda's hand and must have fallen asleep. A soft hand on her hair rustled her out of a restless sleep. The realization of where she was made her lift her head. She blinked, clearing her vision to find her dear friend smiling at her.

"Long day, kid?" Wanda asked in her familiar gravelly voice.

Caitlin pushed to her feet and gently hugged Wanda, then sat back down. "How do you feel?"

"Like I got run over by an eighteen-wheeler." She frowned. "I could really go for a smoke."

Caitlin smiled. Wanda was definitely back.

"The nurse told me you don't remember what happened." Caitlin held her breath expectantly.

Wanda ran her hand over her face, careful not to dislodge the oxygen line running under her nose. She shifted her eyes toward the door without moving her head, then returned her gaze to Caitlin. "He's been watching me like a hawk."

Caitlin furrowed her brows.

"The sheriff. Is he out in the hall?"

"No, the nurse said he left." She decided she'd wait to tell her about her boyfriend's suspected involvement in the drug trafficking activities at the compound. There was still so much they had to unravel, and there was no sense bothering Wanda about it right now.

Wanda reached up and clutched her hand. "I lied about not remembering what happened."

Caitlin's blood ran cold.

"And I'm going to keep lying until I can get out of this hospital bed and home to my guns so I can protect myself."

Caitlin tilted her head, waiting for Wanda to continue.

"That SOB—the sheriff," she added, in case it wasn't clear who she was talking about, "tried to tell me you had gone off the rails. That you were obsessed with the compound. He wanted to know what you said. He knew we were meeting for breakfast and told me to stay home. When I refused, he pushed me hard. That's the last thing I remember."

"Oh, I'm so sorry." Emotion clogged her throat.

"Nothing for you to be sorry about." Wanda winced as if something hurt. "Good thing I realized who he was before I wasted any more time with his sorry self."

"Wait, how did he know you were supposed to meet me for breakfast?" Caitlin understood if her friend had confided in the man she had grown close to. Caitlin already found herself sharing things with Austin, a man she had just met but grown close to over a very short time.

"I've been thinking about that a lot today since I regained consciousness. I think he was worried about what you were up to and he used me to get information on you. I'm not sure how he knew about our breakfast."

"I'm sorry you got hurt on account of me."

The older woman squeezed her hand. "Not because of you. You don't control anyone's choices." Wanda met her gaze. This was something she had been telling Caitlin since they first met across the phone line all those years ago. A maternal 911 dispatcher and a scared ten-year-old who couldn't get her mother to choose her over men, drinks, and nights out.

Caitlin nodded, unable to find the words.

"One of these days you're going to believe me." Wanda closed her eyes, obviously tired.

"I hate to interrupt." Austin appeared at the door. "I got my supervisor to authorize two agents to look for Chris Rutherford on Solomon's property. At dawn."

"Your supervisor?" Wanda asked, confusion narrowing her eyes. "Who do you work for?"

"The FBI."

"Ahh…" A small smile tilted Wanda's lips as she shifted her gaze to Caitlin. "So your new friend isn't part of that compound. That's good news."

Caitlin couldn't help but chuckle. "I suppose it is." Her gaze drifted from her sweet friend's to Austin's. Feeling flustered at the attention, she said, "What about…" she let her words trail off and glanced around. She didn't want to overwhelm Wanda while she was recovering. "Everything else. At the compound."

"That's going to take more proof. But we'll get it." Austin seemed to be holding something back.

"Well, we have enough proof to arrest the sheriff." Caitlin tipped her head toward Wanda. "For assault, for starters."

"I'll have an agent interview you when you're ready," Austin said. "Tomorrow?"

"I'm not going anywhere." Wanda let out a long sigh. "Now go. I need some sleep."

CHAPTER 39

"You don't need to be here." Austin flipped up his collar against the brisk wind. The beep-beep-beeping of the recovery equipment bounced across the Redman land as the sun rose on a new day. He was glad they got an early start because the weather was supposed to turn.

The day Austin would finally get the answer he dreaded.

"I want to be here." Caitlin took a step closer, and her presence alone calmed his rioting emotions. He had called Janelle Rutherford late last night to tell her the news. She sounded resigned. Her little brother had been missing for a long time.

Austin swallowed around a lump in his throat. "It's okay if you want to go see Wanda in the hospital."

"It's covered. Olivia is with her. Drew had the day off from work, so he'll be home with his daughter."

"You have some solid friends," Austin said, considering how his life had been a mostly lonely pursuit.

"I do." They locked gazes.

A commotion at the well drew their attention. "I think

they found something," Austin said. As if in a trance, he moved toward the well and looked at the images on the monitor sent up from the bottom of the well. A decomposing body in the same coat as the photo he had been showing around. His heart sank.

The man working the equipment said, "We'll get him up."

Austin gave a quick nod. Then he tuned into his phone vibrating in his pocket. He slid it out. One of his fellow agents.

"We got it," the excited agent's voice sounded over the phone. Things were happening fast.

Austin stepped away from the well and did a fist pump. "What happens now?"

"They're moving in quick. They are working on the warrant now."

"Okay, okay." Austin's mind was racing. "Where is the meeting point?"

"I'm sorry, Austin, you have to sit this one out. All things considered."

"Yeah." *All things considered.* He had gone out solo on this mission to find Chris Rutherford. He wouldn't be allowed back on active duty until he was cleared.

If he was cleared. For some reason, the thought didn't alarm him as much as it should.

"Go do your thing. Keep me posted."

"Will do," his fellow agent said.

Austin lowered the phone and directed Caitlin to the edge of the property out of earshot of anyone else. Her bright blue eyes studied him. "What is it?"

"US Customs and Border Protection stopped one of Clyde Wheeler's trucks at the Peace Bridge headed into Canada." He raised his eyebrows. "Based on a tip. They found cocaine in a false bottom on the truck." Thanks to Elmer, they knew exactly where to search.

"Wow…"

"They're assembling a team, and they're going to raid the compound this morning." Austin leaned in and gave her an impulsive kiss.

"You did it." She cupped his cheek and smiled.

He shook his head. "I couldn't have done it without you."

Caitlin took a step back. "Go ahead and meet your team. I'll stay here."

"No, I have to sit this one out." He released a quick breath. "My punishment for going rogue."

"It was bound to happen." She gave him a rueful smile, but a warm light shone in her eyes.

"This was a price I was willing to pay to find Chris. To bring closure to his family."

CHAPTER 40

Caitlin had her hand hooked around Austin's arm in the blowing snow. The Hunters Ridge medical examiner loaded the body of Chris Rutherford into the back of his station wagon. After the red taillights were swallowed up in the gathering snowstorm, Caitlin nudged him. "It's time to go."

Austin nodded. He patted her hand. "Thank you for being here for me."

"Of course." Caitlin tugged down on her hat and felt an overwhelming sense of sadness. For a young man's life cut short. For whatever this was between her and Austin about to end before it really had a chance to blossom.

"Come on. We should get to the hospital," Austin said. "Check on Wanda."

"Olivia called a little while ago. They released Wanda and she agreed to go home with her. She'll be safe there if the sheriff gets any ideas."

"Good."

They climbed into the cab of his truck, and Caitlin rubbed her gloves together. Austin fired up the engine and got the heat going. The wipers swept off the new dusting of snow. Austin's phone rang and he answered it over speaker. It was one of the FBI agents on the compound.

"Clyde Wheeler has a massive operation out of one of the buildings in back. This is huge. *Huge*. They're taking everyone in. It's going to take some time to sort out."

Austin's jaw clenched. "Okay, okay…"

"But one thing. Wheeler wasn't on the compound."

Caitlin's stomach dropped at the information.

"Are you sure?" Austin bit out the question.

"It's a big piece of property. We're combing it now."

Austin cleared his throat. "Thanks for letting me know." He ended the call and muttered, "Darn it."

"Let's head in that direction. No one's going to stop us from watching the surrounding roads," Caitlin suggested.

Austin slanted her a half-smile. "I knew I liked you."

"The feeling is mutual." She reached up over her shoulder and yanked the seat belt in place. "Let's go."

Austin jammed his truck into drive and the tires took a hot second to gain purchase. They drove toward the compound. A slow-moving buggy was hugging the edge of the road. "Man, I'd hate to be out in these elements."

"The storm must have caught them off guard." She turned to see if she recognized the driver as they passed, but his black coat and hat were universal in Hunters Ridge.

A vehicle was approaching them head on, and Austin had to cut the steering wheel to get out of the way. "He's coming pretty fast," Austin muttered. "Slow down, buddy, or you'll end up in a ditch."

Caitlin was tracking the advancing car when prickles of awareness made her heart race. "Wait, that Jeep. I've seen it up at the compound." The driver was a male with a baseball cap pulled low. He kept his attention directly ahead of him. A thrill coursed through her. "That's him. That's Wheeler!"

"Are you sure?" Austin asked. Without waiting for confirmation, he did a wide U-turn and fell in pursuit. That's when the driver sped up. "It's him all right. No other reason to try to outrun us."

Caitlin pulled out her weapon, checked it, then set it on her lap, facing the passenger door. She looked up and had to squint against the fast-falling snow. The wipers couldn't keep up. The engine revved.

"Slow up, there's a sharp curve at the top of this road," Caitlin warned Austin.

He did as she said, but the vehicle ahead of them wasn't as cautious. The Jeep bobbled over the edge of the road and down an embankment.

"Oh, no!" she breathed.

"Idiot," he muttered under his breath.

The back of Austin's truck fishtailed as he pulled over in the deep snow. "Stay here," he said as he pushed open the driver's side door.

Caitlin watched as he strode in front of the vehicle and followed the tire tracks through the freshly fallen snow. She slowly opened the passenger door, then walked around the other side of the truck for cover. She found herself saying a silent prayer for Austin's safety. The second time in recent days after years of ignoring her faith. It had fallen by the wayside the night her mother died. In all the years since, she had found it fruitless. Or perhaps she hadn't realized how much she had to be thankful for.

Caitlin pressed down her hat and lifted her hood against the elements. Holding the gun in her cold hands, she waited. Whatever came at her, she'd be ready.

Austin navigated the snowy incline following the tracks made by the Jeep, his boots sinking into the deep snow. He trained his focus on the back end of the Jeep, not sure if the driver was alert and ready for anything. Austin held his gun, waiting.

About ten feet off the rear driver's side of the vehicle, he couldn't make anything out in the side-view mirror. "Put your hands where I can see them!"

No response. He inched closer, the wind-whipped snow hampering his vision. Adrenaline surged through his veins, in stark contrast to the icy wind slicing across his exposed face.

"FBI," Austin said, finally getting Wheeler in his sights. "Don't move."

The man turned his head. Blood trickled down his forehead.

Taking advantage of his dazed state, Austin yanked open the door. "Clyde Wheeler, you're under arrest for transporting drugs across international borders."

Wheeler slowly blinked. "I knew you weren't who you said you were."

"You should have trusted your gut," Austin said as he pulled the man out of the vehicle, handcuffed and shoved him to the top of the incline. When he reached the truck, he smiled when he saw Caitlin armed and ready to be his backup.

She approached them. "Is he hurt?"

"I think he'll be fine."

"Take me into the sheriff's station," Wheeler said. "Littlefield will straighten everything out."

"The sheriff has his own problems to sort out," Caitlin said.

Wheeler cussed under his breath.

Austin sat Wheeler down on the snowy berm. He pulled

out his phone. "I'll call for someone to pick him up. And to get this Jeep out of the ditch."

Caitlin nodded. "You want to make a statement while we're here?"

"I'm not talking to anyone. This is all crap." His open jacket flapped in the wind with his hands fastened behind him. His cheeks burned bright red and icicles formed on the tips of his sweaty hair.

Austin grabbed his elbow. "Let's get you out of the elements."

Despite the man's protests, they stuffed him in the back seat of Austin's truck until the FBI SUV arrived.

A fellow FBI agent took custody and said, "Maybe this will win you some points with the supervisor in charge."

Austin laughed. "We'll see. Thanks." Then he jerked his chin toward Wheeler's vehicle. "Someone going to come get the Jeep?"

The agent nodded. "Yeah, impound it."

"Thanks."

He climbed back into his truck where Caitlin waited for him, holding her hands up to the warm heating vents.

"All set?" she asked.

"Yeah, I think I am." Austin put the truck into drive and cut her a curious gaze. "Where to now?"

"Someplace warm."

CHAPTER 41

When Austin and Caitlin had arrived at his cabin last night, a slew of FBI agents were waiting for him. So they'd said their goodbyes—not how she had planned—and one of the agents, after debriefing her, drove her home. Now, she had a message on her cell phone from Austin that he was headed back to Buffalo to talk to his supervisor.

So that was that.

Caitlin shoved aside the disappointment and headed over to Olivia's to check on Wanda, who had been released from the hospital and went home with her dear friend. When Caitlin arrived, Wanda, Olivia and baby Charlotte were sitting in the kitchen having coffee. For the first time since she had met Wanda, the older woman didn't have a cigarette pinched between her fingers with her morning coffee.

Olivia greeted Caitlin with a tight embrace. "Just my luck, all the good stuff goes on while I'm on maternity leave."

"I'm sure there'll be more crime when you get back," Caitlin said, and the three women all laughed.

"Let's hope so. I like my job," Wanda said.

"I hope you're going to take a little time off," Caitlin said. "How do you feel?"

"Much better since that jerk is in custody."

The agent that drove Caitlin home last night had said the sheriff had been picked up at his home. Caitlin couldn't help but think about the man. A lifetime in law enforcement and this was going to be his legacy: a lookout for a man trafficking drugs in and out of Canada. That was going to be a lot of years in prison, probably his remaining days.

"Did anyone have any idea he was involved with this?" Olivia asked in a singsong voice, both soothing the baby in her arms and asking the question they were all wondering.

"None," Wanda said.

"He was always rough around the edges, especially when dealing with the Amish. He always acted like they were a bother. And he often treated some of his deputies the same way." Especially her and Olivia. Caitlin poured herself a cup of coffee and plunked down at the kitchen table. "But I had no idea he was breaking the law he had pledged to uphold."

"Well, he'll get what's coming to him," Olivia said, rubbing the baby's back.

"I'm sorry your relationship didn't work out," Caitlin said to Wanda.

"Good riddance. I'm glad to be rid of him. Can you believe that jerk bugged my house?" Wanda asked, most likely grasping onto every grievance to soothe her hurt feelings. Harder to miss the guy when she kept reminding herself what a jerk he was.

Surprise zinged through Caitlin. "That's how he knew you and I had breakfast scheduled? That's why he confronted you?"

"Exactly. Jerk," Wanda muttered. "I asked Deputy Kimble to search my house last night. He found it partially hidden by the rug."

"The sheriff probably put it under the table and when he went to retrieve it, couldn't find it. Nice break." Wanda took another sip of coffee and winced.

"Are you okay?" Caitlin asked.

Wanda nodded. "Just missing my nicotine fix." She waved her hand, as if someone had offered her one. "I'm going to kick that habit. If Littlefield can't take me out, I'm not going to let that habit kill me." Caitlin smiled and Wanda jabbed a finger in her direction. "I don't want to hear anything from you, thank you very much."

Caitlin mimed that she was locking her lips shut and throwing away the key.

"Where's Austin?" Olivia asked, changing the subject. "I knew when I invited you both to dinner that you'd hit it off."

Caitlin pointed to her locked lips, and they all laughed.

"No way are you going to stay tight-lipped on that one," Wanda said. "He is one hot man."

Caitlin couldn't help but smile. Then she grew somber. "He suffered a blow. The young man they found in the well was like a brother to him. Wheeler had him killed after perceiving him as a threat to his business."

"That's tough," Olivia said, adjusting the baby's blanket over her back. "I'm sure you'll be able to help him through his loss."

Caitlin shook her head. "No, no, we were just working together. That's all."

"That's all," Wanda mimicked her.

"Besides, he already went back to Buffalo." She fought to keep the disappointment from her voice. "Work called him back for an urgent meeting. I'll probably never see him again."

Olivia lifted an eyebrow as if to say, *We'll see.*

"Hmmm..." Wanda said. "Anyone want to take any bets on that?"

CHAPTER 42

ne week later

Caitlin tried not to feel hurt when Austin didn't reach out to her in the days after he left. They had been together for less than a week, but they had packed a lot in that one week. However, when she received a call from Janelle Rutherford, Chris's sister, Caitlin realized she had to put aside her hurt feelings. So she hopped into her SUV and drove the short distance to Buffalo, timing her arrival—per Janelle's suggestion—for right after the funeral.

The butterflies in Caitlin's stomach grew more frantic as she approached the black-and-white checkered flag on her GPS screen. When it announced, "Your destination is on the right," she pulled over and sat, unsure if she was doing the right thing. Her mother had always chased guys, and they treated her horribly. Caitlin had spent her adult life independent, and this whole situation was foreign to her.

After taking a moment to catch her breath, she shut off

the engine and climbed out in the gray slushy snow. Double-checking the house number, she strode up to the neat white house. She cleared her throat and lifted her hand to knock.

Footsteps sounded inside, and in that moment her heartbeat exploded. *Too late to run.* Well, not if she didn't want him to see her retreating to her vehicle. That would have been more embarrassing than accepting her fate.

The locks clicked and the doorknob rattled. The door swung open and a handsome man with a clean-shaven face, in a dark suit, appeared in the doorway. His expression grew slack, perhaps taking a moment to process the situation.

Caitlin lifted her hand. "I should have called." Janelle had encouraged her to show up unannounced. Now, she could clearly see that was a bad idea in the stormy clouds in his eyes. A whoosh of shame heated her face and she wanted to melt into the sidewalk.

What was I thinking?

Austin pushed open the door and the storm clouds parted. His mouth remained grim, but the spark of something more lit his eyes. "Come here." His gravelly voice washed over her and sent tingles racing through her. She took a step forward, and he reached for her hand and brought her into the small foyer and pulled her into a fierce hug.

"I was worried about you," Caitlin said into his chest. He smelled of aloe and Tide.

"I was worried about me, too." A soft laugh vibrated through his throat against the side of her head.

"Did you lose your job?" She pulled back a fraction, and he loosened his grip on her.

Austin shook his head. "A slap on the wrist." At that moment, he swept his thumb across her exposed wrist at the cuff on her thick winter coat. "My supervisor wasn't happy, but in the end, a major drug trafficking operation was taken down, so..."

"The ends justify the means," Caitlin said casually, despite every nerve ending being on fire.

"I'll serve some sort of punishment to prevent the other agents from 'getting ideas.'" He did a single-hand air quote. "I'm really not worried about it," he added.

She dipped her head, then looked up and met his gaze. "Are you okay? Really?"

"Did Janelle call you?"

Caitlin nodded.

With his one free hand, Austin rubbed the back of his neck. "I feel like I let Chris down. He never had much of a father figure. Then, when I ran off to the army, he felt abandoned."

"Janelle told me you were a wonderful influence on him. You have to hold on to the good memories."

Austin's lips twitched. "I try."

"I've been working hard on not feeling responsible for other people's actions, too." Her guilt over her mother's death would probably be a lifetime of therapy sessions.

Austin nodded, then seemed to snap out of it. "Here, let me take your coat." He helped her out of her coat, then led her to the kitchen where he had just made himself something to eat. "I just got home from the funeral. Can I make you something?"

"No, I'm fine." She was too nervous to be hungry. She sat down across from him and they discussed the arrests, the potential punishment for the key players, and the rumors about what would happen to the compound now that Wheeler was in custody. The property would probably remain vacant like it had for years prior to Wheeler buying it. The men who had worked there had been rounded up and charges were being filed. The Amish, who were innocent, would likely return to their family's farms, or take off on another adventure.

"What's the word on Elmer?" Austin asked.

"His mother told me that the lawyer said he might serve less time in prison because of his cooperation. He had been on probation and has a record. And he helped load the trucks. He was part of the operation." She ran her palm across the smooth wood of the table. "But I think he'll come out a better person. I hope."

"Yeah, I do too." Austin pushed his plate aside.

"So when do you go back to work?" Caitlin finally asked.

"Monday."

"Oh…" Caitlin wasn't sure what she'd expected.

"But I'm not sure I'm going to go back."

Austin's confession sent a jolt of adrenaline coursing through her, but she couldn't form any words.

"I have to clean up and sell my parents' house. That should take some time. I have a little money saved, so I'm not worried." He laughed, a mirthless sound. "When I was out in my dad's workshop, it reminded me how much he loved working with his hands. He made beautiful furniture and made repairs around the house on weekends and evenings. When he could squeeze it in. He, too, was in the FBI." He grimaced. "He always talked about what he'd do when he had time." He drew in a deep breath and let it out. "Well, that day never came. He died when he was fifty."

"So young."

"Yeah. After sorting my dad's tools—and after Chris's murder—it really drove home that nothing is promised." He waved his hand in dismissal. "I'm not making any sense."

"Yes, you are. We live like we have all the time in the world." Caitlin had never thought the last time she saw her mother would be the last time.

"I'm sorry I never called after I left Hunters Ridge." Austin frowned. "I helped Chris's family plan his funeral and—"

"I understand. You don't need to explain anything to me."

Something flashed in his eyes, and he shifted his head to train them on her. "Why did you come today?"

"I thought you might need support." She smiled tightly. "And I wanted to be the one to provide it." She felt like she was laying her soul bare. Her pulse roared in her ears. She couldn't possibly imagine how horrible rejection would feel right now. She wouldn't allow herself.

She had to trust.

Austin took her hand and pulled her into a standing position. "After I finish with my parents' estate, I was thinking about buying Sanders' house I was renting in Hunters Ridge, fixing it up, and selling it." He shrugged. "Or living in it. I guess it depends."

"Depends on what?" Caitlin's mouth felt like chalk.

Austin took a step closer. "How things go with us."

Caitlin glanced down at their joined hands between them. "That's a lot of pressure. I've never…"

"I don't want you to feel the pressure. Not at all. But if I move to Hunters Ridge to fix the house, it'll provide time for us to get to know each other. To explore this"—he gestured in the small space between them—"whatever this is." He released her hands. He slid his hands around her back and pulled her into a tight embrace.

She lifted her head to meet his warm lips.

After a moment, he broke away. "What do you think? No pressure."

"I think it sounds wonderful." Caitlin cupped his clean-shaven cheek. He looked so darn handsome, with or without a beard. "How long before you move to Hunters Ridge?"

"After I sell this house, but I want to declutter it first."

Caitlin looked around the quaint kitchen with all the knickknacks and personal items. "Need help?"

Half his mouth quirked into a wide grin. "I'd love the help."

Caitlin pushed up on her tiptoes and brushed another kiss across his lips. "Because the sooner you're done here, the sooner you'll move to Hunters Ridge."

"Sounds like a plan." He planted a soft kiss on her lips, then pulled away and smiled. "Maybe one of the best ones I've ever had."

～

Dear Reader,

Thank you for reading **Plain Survival.** *I've enjoyed writing the Hunters Ridge Series of Amish romantic suspense. Next up is Tessa and Sawyer's story in* **Plain Inferno.**

It all started with a spark...

With no means to support herself, a pregnant Tessa Sutter is forced to move back to her Amish childhood home on bended knee after her *Englisch* husband goes missing. When her husband's brother, Sawyer King, returns to Hunters Ridge to search for his brother, it soon becomes apparent that whatever Tessa's husband was involved with may have ensnared her. The pair fight their growing attraction while Sawyer is determined to keep Tessa safe.

Read today: Plain Inferno, Book 6 in the Hunters Ridge series

Happy reading,
Alison Stone

ALSO BY ALISON STONE

The Thrill of Sweet Suspense Series

(Stand-alone novels that can be read in any order)

Random Acts

Too Close to Home

Critical Diagnosis

Grave Danger

The Art of Deception

Hunters Ridge: Amish Romantic Suspense

The Millionaire's Amish Bride: Hunters Ridge Amish Romance

Plain Obsession: Book 1

Plain Missing: Book 2

Plain Escape: Book 3

Plain Revenge: Book 4

Plain Survival: Book 5

Plain Inferno: Book 6

Plain Trouble: Book 7

Plain Secrets: Book 8

A Jayne Murphy Dance Academy Cozy Mystery

Pointe & Shoot

Final Curtain

Corpse de Ballet

Bargain Boxed Sets

Hunters Ridge Book Bundle (Books 1-3)

The Thrill of Sweet Suspense Book Bundle (Books 1-3)

For a complete list of books visit

Alison Stone's Amazon Author Page

ABOUT THE AUTHOR

Alison Stone is a *Publishers Weekly bestselling author* who writes sweet romance, cozy mysteries, and inspirational romantic suspense, some of which contain bonnets and buggies.

Alison often refers to herself as the "accidental Amish author." She decided to try her hand at the genre after an editor put a call out for more Amish romantic suspense. Intrigued—and who doesn't love the movie *Witness* with Harrison Ford?—Alison dug into research, including visits to the Amish communities in Western New York where she lives. This sparked numerous story ideas, the first leading to her debut novel with Harlequin Love Inspired Suspense. Four subsequent Love Inspired Suspense titles went on to earn *RT magazine's TOP PICK!* designation, their highest ranking.

When Alison's not plotting ways to bring mayhem to Amish communities, she's writing romantic suspense with a more modern setting, sweet romances, and cozy mysteries. In order to meet her deadlines, she has to block the internet and hide her smartphone.

Married and the mother of four (almost) grown kids, Alison lives in the suburbs of Buffalo where the summers are gorgeous and the winters are perfect for curling up with a book—or writing one.

Be the first to learn about new books, giveaways and deals in Alison's newsletter. Sign up at AlisonStone.com.
Connect with Alison Stone online:
www.AlisonStone.com
Alison@AlisonStone.com

Made in United States
Troutdale, OR
02/27/2024

18038746R00136